LAST CHANCE

This Large Print Book carries the
Seal of Approval of N.A.V.H.

LAST CHANCE

CATHY MARIE HAKE

THORNDIKE PRESS
A part of Gale, Cengage Learning

GALE
CENGAGE Learning™

Detroit • New York • San Francisco • New Haven, Conn • Waterville, Maine • London

GALE
CENGAGE Learning™

Thorndike Press® Large Print Christian Historical Fiction.
The text of this Large Print edition is unabridged.
Other aspects of the book may vary from the original edition.
Set in 16 pt. Plantin.
Printed on permanent paper.

LIBRARY OF CONGRESS CATALOGING-IN-PUBLICATION DATA

Hake, Cathy Marie.
 Last chance / by Cathy Marie Hake.
  p. cm. — (Thorndike Press large print Christian historical fiction.) (Kansas chances ; bk. 1)
 ISBN-13: 978-1-4104-0451-0 (hardcover : alk. paper)
 ISBN-10: 1-4104-0451-X (hardcover : alk. paper)
 1. Large type books. I. Title.
 PS3608.A5454L37 2008
 813'.6—dc22   2007047097

Published in 2008 by arrangement with Barbour Publishing, Inc.

Printed in the United States of America
1 2 3 4 5 6 7 12 11 10 09 08

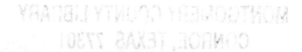

To Genevieve O'Brien.
She reared her younger brothers and
sisters, crossed the United States in a
covered wagon, killed snakes and cooked
them, and became a nurse. Unable to
have children of her own, she legally
adopted one boy. She also opened her
heart to my mom when Dad was
overseas in the service and became
"Grandma Peggy" to us kids in the fullest,
most loving sense of the word.

CHAPTER 1

Salt Lick Holler, Kentucky, June 1872

"I cain't have it. No, I cain't." Silk Trevor stood on the rickety porch of her shack and hung on to either side of the doorsill like a crawdad with juicy bait in both pincers. "You go on ahead and leave my kin here."

Lovejoy Spencer set down her battered canvas valise and carefully unhinged the troublesome brass clasp. She'd expected Silk to kick up a fuss. The strap securing her dulcimer to her back slashed taut across her bosom as she crouched, but the real tightness in her chest came from thinking the whole arrangement might fall apart if Silk didn't cooperate. Drawing a jar from the valise, Lovejoy whispered, "Lord, have mercy and let this work."

After rising and taking a step closer, she held out her offering. "Blackberry jam, Miz Silk — my special recipe. I reckon it'll take away a wee bit of the bitterness of the day.

Each time you spread a dab on that delicious bread of yourn, you cain think on how you've sent yore nieces off to a better life."

Silk's tears miraculously stopped. Her eyes narrowed. "You think a half-pint's all the both of them are worth?"

"All the gold in heaven wouldn't begin to buy such fine young gals," Lovejoy responded without hesitation. "Fact is, I'm not buying them. Jesus ransomed their souls from Lucifer."

"Glory be!" Silk let go of the doorjamb and lifted her hands in praise.

"And there's not a body in all of Salt Lick Holler who doesn't know you've done right by Eunice and Lois. The MacPhersons from up at Hawk's Fall remembered them and honored your family by sending a bridal offer."

Tempy stepped up and nodded. "My sister's right, Miz Silk. Why, everyone here in Salt Lick and folks clear up at Hawk's Fall are all going to ponder on what a wondrous thing you did, rearing Eunice and Lois so the MacPhersons kept pining after them even after moving clear across the country."

It took considerable effort for Lovejoy to keep from flashing her baby sister a smile. At eighteen, Tempy was smart as a whip. If she tried, the girl could likely charm a snake into a knot. From the way Silk perked up, Lovejoy knew her sister had hit the right note.

She chimed in, "Abner MacPherson set all of Salt Lick into a dither when he rode over from Hawk's Fall to deliver the greenbacks. His boys have been sending money home regular-like and still had enough to buy not one, but three train tickets. Bucks like them could snap up any woman, but they picked your nieces."

"Now it's a fact, they did," Silk granted.

"That's sayin' plenty," Lovejoy continued. "They're bright young women, and you've always done what's best for them."

Silk let out a woebegone sigh. "You truly aim to go along, Lovejoy Spencer? I don't want my girls out in that wild world on their own."

"I give you my word. I'll travel the whole way. They'll be married right and tight to good men who'll provide well for them."

Silk nodded. "I reckon that's the best a body could hope for." The minute she plodded out of the doorway, Eunice and Lois hustled out with a trunk betwixt themselves. Pa didn't get down from the buckboard to help, but no one really expected him to. Lovejoy and Tempy helped hoist the trunk onto the wagon bed; then hugs, kisses, and the blackberry jam were traded. They all piled on, and Pa drove them to the pass.

Not a yard went by that Lovejoy didn't study with a mixture of sadness and joy. Spring brought a bounty of healing yarbs. As a healer, Lovejoy knew a wealth of uses for each plant. Smelly as they were, the wild leeks they called ramps could cure many a complaint. Coltsfoot, teaberry, burdock — each belonged in her healing arsenal. Gathering as much as she could of those and dozens upon dozens of other plants in these last few weeks, Lovejoy hoped she'd stored up enough for when she returned.

And she would return to the raw beauty of Kentucky. But she'd be leaving her beloved baby sister clear off in Californy. *'Tis a good life a-waitin' her. I'll dwell on that thought.*

The train wasn't supposed to stop at the pass. Then again, once a week Pa just happened to be sitting there waiting. He'd hand up jugs of moonshine, empty jugs got passed back down, and he'd leave with a smile and a pocketful of cash money.

Last week he'd arranged for the girls to ride clear across these United States to San Francisco, then for the stage ride to Reliable where the MacPhersons lived. He'd

10

groused at the cost as if he'd paid for the tickets himself. When Lovejoy announced she was going as a chaperone, he flatly refused to pay for her.

She'd not given in, though.

Her baby sister was about to be a bride. So were Eunice and Lois. The MacPherson brothers had written a letter asking the three gals to come out and do them the honor of becoming their wives. Truth was, Lovejoy determined to go along regardless of the cost. These young gals weren't going to marry up with the MacPhersons unless the men passed her muster.

She'd been bound in a marriage that brought nothing but misery. Long as she drew breath, she refused to let Tempy — or any gal — get roped into matrimony if all it would become was a noose.

Being a widow woman of the ripe age of four-and-twenty, Lovejoy didn't answer to any man. Added to that, she owned a small place and was a trained granny-woman. Folks came to her for all sorts of other healing, too. Chickens, cheese, a bottle of molasses — her patients paid however and whatever they could afford. Hardscrabble as they lived, it amounted to precious little. That being the case, the notion that Tempy, Eunice, and Lois might have a better life out in Californy made Lovejoy pry up the floorboard and pull out the precious stash of coins she kept in a coffee can for a rainy day.

Stooped with age, Widow Hendricks reckoned she'd be able to fill in for a season as the healer — seein' as that season would be warm and dry. With the dear Lord providing enough money for Lovejoy to make the trip and someone to tend the folks back home, she felt certain it was His will for her to go.

When Pa realized he'd not stop her, he'd gone off and gotten roostered on his own 'shine. Years ago, Lovejoy had Tempy move in with her, and Pa had a habit of showing up at suppertime more often than not. His other daughters — married and up to their hips in young'uns — never had a place for him at their tables. Lovejoy's only rule was that she wouldn't open her door to him if he was drunk. He'd shown up that night reeking of the devil's brew and making wild threats. If anything, that only strengthened her resolve. Lovejoy wanted her sister away from this.

Now at the pass, Pa jerked the trunk and satchels off the wagon — more out of the need to reach his moonshine than to be a gentleman. He lined up the jugs and helped

12

himself to a stiff belt of who-hit-John from the flask he habitually carried. "You oughtn't tag along," he said to Lovejoy.

Her stomach roiled when she caught a whiff of his fetid breath. She dug in her heels. "Mama put Tempy under my wing back on the day she was born."

"Your ma woulda done better to give me sons 'stead of a passel of girls." He took another swig.

"I know you loved her in your own way, Pa. God rest her soul, Mama loved you back." Mama had turned a blind eye to Pa's still because it was the only way they could put food on the table. By the time Lovejoy was sixteen, Pa married her off to Vern Spencer. Jug-bit men did foolish things, and both Pa and Vern did their share of drinking. Lovejoy still believed Pa was a good man when he wasn't drinking; just two days after Vern took her to wife, she knew she couldn't say the same for him. The four years of marriage that followed felt like forty.

The metal rail by Lovejoy's toe started to vibrate. "Train'll be here in a minute."

Pa nodded. The train always moved slowly through the winding hills and hollers, so stopping wasn't all that difficult. Once it came to a standstill, he held the gals back. "First things first." He took care of his illegal business transaction, then let them board the train. He wiped a tear from his weathered cheek after he gave Tempy a bear hug and lifted her onto the train steps. Lovejoy stepped forward, stood on tiptoe, and gave him a kiss, too.

"You really goin' through with this foolish plan of yourn?" he whispered gruffly.

"I've gotta, Pa."

"Then go." He crammed real paper money into her hand and shoved her onto the train.

Chance Ranch, Reliable, California

"Pretty as a princess," Daniel Chance recited as he pulled his comb through little Polly's hair. "Your mama was pretty as can be. Hair as soft and light as a moonbeam."

"Just like mine," his daughter said gleefully.

Polly never tired of hearing about her mama, and Dan wanted his daughters to grow up knowing what an extraordinary woman she'd been. It was part of their morning ritual, and it gave Daniel an opportunity to cherish his memories and pass them along. Just after the birth of their second daughter, Hannah passed on and took most of his heart with her. What little was left, he devoted entirely to his daughters.

Daniel continued to comb the waves left by her nighttime braids. One of his sisters-in-law would plait Polly's hair after breakfast. His big hands were made for chopping wood and branding cattle — not for braiding cornsilk-fine hair on a wiggly four-year-old.

"Mama in heben." Two-year-old Ginny Mae curled her toes on the cold floor and leaned into him for warmth.

"Yes. Mama's in heaven." Dan strove to keep his tone even. "Polly, go get your shoes and socks. Bring Ginny's, too."

Polly scampered through the "hall" to the adjoining cabin. The Chance brothers had connected the two cabins so Daniel would have sufficient space. He'd refused to move out of the little cabin he and his beloved Hannah shared, but it grew far too cramped with the girls' bed. They didn't have enough room to turn around without tripping over something or bumping into each other. The girls' cabin boasted a loft and a bit more room, but more important, it had a potbellied stove so it stayed warmer.

Daniel pulled Ginny Mae onto his lap and warmed her tiny feet in his hands. "Piggy, Daddy!"

"This little piggy went to market. . . ."

Polly came back carrying Ginny's shoes

15

and one sock and wearing her own shoes on the wrong feet. "Sissy gots only one sock, Daddy. I can't find the other one."

Daniel grimaced. Ginny had had an accident last evening, and he'd intended to wash out the wet sock. Somehow he'd gotten distracted. "She'll wear one today."

Polly fidgeted as he slipped the sock and first shoe on her sister. Suddenly, she pointed at Ginny Mae's feet and sing-songed, "Diddle, diddle dumplin', my son John, went to bed with his trousers on."

"I a girl," Ginny protested. "I no wear tr'srs."

"One shoe off and one shoe on," Polly sang louder.

"She has both shoes on now." Daniel stood and set her down. He took a moment to make his bed — not because he thought it important, but if he didn't, Miriam, Alisa, or Delilah would do it. He didn't want his sisters-in-law doing more on his behalf. They already did his laundry, stitched his girls' sweet little dresses, and minded his daughters. Much as he hated being beholden to them, he had no choice.

Besides, making the bed killed a few more minutes. He didn't like showing up to breakfast until it was on the table. Though he didn't begrudge his brothers their happy marriages, it hurt something fierce to stand by and watch them and their wives radiating early morning contentment. To their credit, they'd not pushed him to remarry, and they put up with his curt ways. Dan did his best to shield his daughters from his grief, but it took everything he had to do just that. Fortunately, the girls' aunts and uncles stepped in and doted on them to help fill in the empty spaces in their young hearts and lives. As soon as he wolfed down his breakfast and kissed his daughters, he could escape for the day. No matter how hard the work, though, he never managed to escape the soul-deep emptiness that plagued him since Hannah went to the hereafter.

"No need to waste good cash money on hiring a ride," Lovejoy Spencer said to her charges. "We'll walk. It's only seven miles or so."

"But we have our belongings!"

Lovejoy gave Eunice a pat. "I know you're a tad weary. Think on how each step's a-takin' you closer to your intended. That ought to make the load light."

Lois elbowed her sister. "She don't know how much you stuffed in your half of the trunk."

"We need to get directions." Tempy gawked up and down the busy street.

"Easy as fallin' off a log. Never seen so many folks in one place." Lovejoy looked about Reliable and silently compared it to Salt Lick Holler. White's Mercantile looked pert near as fancy as any big city store, and though it was Wednesday, the men all wore their Sunday-go-to-meetin' best.

It would take more than fancy duds to win Lovejoy's approval, though. She was far more concerned with whether the MacPhersons would be steady men and cherish the gals. "We'll get started right quick. I ken yore all eager to meet yore men."

Eunice quavered, "I brought every last thing I own."

Lovejoy smiled at her. "No shame in you bringing along your treasures to turn the house into a home. Now that I think on it, your trunk's right heavy. Mayhap the storekeeper'll know of someone headin' our way."

"It occurs to me, as many strapping men as there are hereabouts" — Lois flashed a smile and waved at a pair of men by the saloon's hitching post — "if things don't work out with the MacPhersons, I'll still be able to find me a husband."

"Last thing you need is a man who likes

his likker." Lovejoy scowled at the men, but to her dismay, they weren't discouraged. They ambled across the road and doffed their hats.

"Good day, ladies." The smooth talker flashed them a smile that would do any snake oil salesman proud. "What a wonder it is to find such a bevy of beauties here in our fair town."

"Nice of you to swap howdies with us, but we're here to meet up with the MacPhersons." Lovejoy stepped forward and sensed Tempy at her side. Between the two of them, they shoved Eunice and Lois behind them. They'd perfected this move by now after five days of travel.

"The MacPhersons?" One of the men hooked his thumbs in his suspenders and craned his neck so he could catch a better view of Lois and Eunice's flame-haired beauty. "My, my. We didn't put much store in their boasts that they had brides coming."

Tempy bristled. "Mike MacPherson's no flannel-mouthed liar!"

"Don't get your back up, miss. He was just making conversation." The first one flashed Tempy that same smile again.

Lovejoy took exception to how he spoke to her sister. Before she could say a thing, the other tacked on, "It's always a pleasure to have available women arrive."

Lovejoy pressed her hand to her bosom and used the other hand to shove Tempy behind herself with the others. "Sir, I'll have you know these are not 'available women.' They're ladies, and they're already bespoken."

"Least they're not getting snapped up by the Chance brothers this time," another man said as he moseyed up.

"We're due at the MacPhersons'." Lovejoy scanned the rapidly growing semicircle of men.

Several men volunteered to take them, but they all seemed too willing. Lovejoy was about to announce they'd walk when a woman came out of the mercantile. She called, "Todd Dorsey's at the blacksmith's. He's the MacPhersons' nearest neighbor. I've sent my husband to fetch Mr. Dorsey. You gals come on in here to wait."

"Much obliged, ma'am." Lovejoy shepherded the girls to safety and knew she'd met an ally when the woman blocked the mercantile door.

"You men get back to your own business. I won't have you pestering these women." She shut the door and turned. "I'm Reba White."

20

Lovejoy introduced her charges and repeated, "Much obliged to you, ma'am. That was quite a pack of curly wolves."

"I promised the MacPhersons and Chances that I'd keep an eye out for you." Reba grinned. "They didn't have to ask. I can't tell you how delighted I am to have a few more good, God-fearing women moving to Reliable."

They didn't have to wait long at the mercantile. Good thing, that. Tempy and Eunice started mooning over every last wondrous, new-fangled thing in the place. Lois satisfied herself by standing at the specialty display case, choosing her favorite wedding band from the three shown there alongside fancy gold pocket watches. Mr. Dorsey loaded the trunk and their satchels on the wagon, and then they all clambered aboard.

About a mile down the road, Mr. Dorsey cleared his throat. "If you all don't mind me stopping off at my place, I can drive you the rest of the way tomorrow."

"It's a mighty fine offer, but we're expected." Tempy smoothed her skirts. "Helping us out even partway was right neighborly of you."

Awhile later, as they stood on the dusty road and waved good-bye to Mr. Dorsey,

Lois said, "He's got mean, beady eyes. I didn't trust him a lick. Good thing you said we wouldn't go home with him!"

"Mrs. White back at the store spoke highly of him." Lovejoy looked at the other fork in the road. "Best we jump to what lies ahead rather than waste time judging what's past."

Another mile down the road, Eunice set down her end of the trunk and wailed, "I cain't do this. It's too heavy."

Dust swirled as Lois dropped her end and plopped down on the trunk. "She's right." Her brow puckered. "If'n the MacPhersons are expectin' us, why didn't they fetch us?"

"I told the truth. They are expecting us. I just didn't say when." Tempy fanned herself.

"Men cain't very well stop everything and go to town each day — leastways, not hardworking ones." Lovejoy stared at the trunk. "This is a genuine opportunity. We'll show them you're just as tireless."

"There!" Lovejoy stood back about half an hour later and surveyed their creation. They'd lashed hickory broomsticks to the ends of the trunk with a length of clothesline rope. "Why, it's just like how they carried the ark of the covenant in the Old Testament."

"I hope it looked better than this," Lois

muttered.

Lovejoy started to laugh. "Sure and enough, it did. After all, our rods are sideways."

"Hope the cherubims don't take offense." Tempy giggled. She pointed to the satchels and valises piled atop the trunk. "The angels' wings are supposed to meet over the ark. That baggage looks more like gargoyles."

"What're gargles?" Eunice scratched her elbow.

"Gargoyles are funny-looking stone critters on old, old churches," Tempy explained patiently.

Lovejoy felt a spurt of pleasure at her sister's book learning. Tempy was better educated than any other woman in Salt Lick. That wasn't saying much, but at moments like this, when Tempy shared her knowledge, Lovejoy knew the sacrifices she'd made on her baby sister's behalf were worth it all.

"So gargoyles are sorta like those dog-ugly wooden owls Otis Nye keeps a-carvin' and setting up on his barn?"

"I never thought of them that way, but you got the drift of it." Tempy looked at Lovejoy. "Reckon we ought to pick this up and step lively."

Each of them took hold of the hickory broom handles and hefted. "Let's sing so we step in time," Lovejoy suggested. She thought for a moment then started in, "We're marching to Zion, beautiful, beautiful Zion. . . ."

The sun had set, and she'd begun to worry that they'd made the wrong decision about which fork to take a mile ago when she spied a group of buildings ahead. "Pony up, gals. The chimney's smokin', and yonder's your future."

The tempo of the hymn and their footsteps picked up. Just as they drew even with the first building, a huge bear of a man stepped from the shadow and blocked their path. "This isn't Zion, so you can just turn around and march the other way."

CHAPTER 2

The short, brown-haired gal closest to him laughed.

Daniel glowered at her.

"Now there speaks a man in sore want of his supper." Merriment rang in her voice. Even in the twilight, her hazel eyes sparkled. As she spoke, she somehow managed to ease something into his hand. A stick.

"If you tell us where to go, we'll be happy to put together something that'll fill your belly."

The stick was attached to an odd affair and carried considerable weight. How a scrap of a woman managed to carry it was beyond him, but Daniel refused to be sidetracked. "Ma'am, I already told you where to go — turn around and march the other way. You'd best be quick about it. It's going dark."

"He's 'bout as friendly as a riled porcupine."

"I'm fixin' to tell my intended to turn him loose and let him find labor elsewhere."

The spunky one up front cut in, "Gals, be charitable. He's probably worked long and hard today." She tried to take the stick back from him.

Daniel refused to let go.

"You cain turn loose now, mister. I brung hale gals. They mebbe tired, but you'll see they don't quail at totin' a fair load."

"Daniel!" Gideon called from a ways off. "Who are you talking to?"

In the slim minutes since he'd met the troop of women, the sky had darkened significantly. Daniel hated admitting defeat, but he couldn't send four defenseless women into the night. "Don't know who they are."

"That other feller don't sound like he's from back home," one of the redheads in the back whispered.

"I'm Lovejoy Spencer, mister. These gals are under my wing. I'm to deliver them to the MacPhersons." She stared up into his eyes and tacked on, "And I'm figurin' we shoulda veered t'other direction back at the road's bend."

"Give me this." He tugged her out of the way and hefted the entire load onto his back. "Gideon, the mail-order brides got

26

turned around. I'm walking them over to the MacPhersons'.""

"Way too late for that. Ladies, come on in. The women are setting supper on the table."

"We don't want to be a bother."

Daniel snorted. "Miss Spencer, it's the nature of women to do just that."

"Pardon Daniel. He's always surly. I'm Gideon Chance."

To Daniel's relief, his brother assumed half the burden. *How were those scrawny little women hauling this?* "We can take this on over to the barn and —"

"The main house," Gideon interrupted. "Ladies, you'd do well to follow along behind us." He raised his voice and called to his wife, "Miriam!"

Daniel didn't move. He squinted at Lovejoy and the woman standing by her side. "The bows and quivers aren't going inside."

"Bows and — oh! 'Tisn't that a'tall. Mine is a dulcimer, and Tempy's toting a mandolin."

"Wonderful," Gideon said as he started walking so Dan had to move to keep from dumping the trunk. "Perhaps you could grace us with a tune or two after supper."

Once they got inside the main house, Dan set down his end of the trunk and turned to get a better look at the women. Miriam and Delilah were making a big fuss over them. The redheads and the one with a mandolin across her back all jostled about the washstand. Lovejoy knelt on the floor on the far side of the table. She had her head tilted to the side and an arm about Polly's shoulders, while gently dabbing at his daughter's runny nose.

"Polly. Ginny Mae." He clapped his hands. "Come to Daddy."

Lovejoy released Polly and nimbly gained her feet. "The Lord shorely blessed you with such lassies, Mr. Chance."

He nodded curtly.

"There are only three MacPhersons; I'm countin' four women." Bryce bit his lip and stared at the gals.

"I'm a widow woman. Came 'long to be sure the girls would be happy. Then I'm a-goin' back home. I'm Lovejoy Spencer. This here's my baby sister, Temperance." She then gestured toward the two gals whose hair matched the color of a terracotta flowerpot. "Eunice and Lois are our neighbors from back home."

Gideon introduced the Chance clan. These gals from the backwoods would probably remember how to tell apart Miriam, Delilah, and Alisa because they were respectively blond, black haired, and in the motherly way. Daniel figured it was an exercise in futility when it came to the strangers recalling his brothers' names.

"You've met Daniel," Gideon yammered on. "Paul is Delilah's husband. Titus is married to Alisa. Logan and Bryce are the young ones."

While folks exchanged pleasantries and carried food to the matched pair of tables, Daniel got waylaid by Ginny Mae for a few minutes. Both of his daughters acted a mite cranky, but with all the hoopla, he wasn't too surprised.

Logan elbowed his way to the table and sat between the redheaded sisters. "Parson Abe preached about Eunice and Lois a few months back. They were in the Bible, you know."

Alisa passed the corn to Lovejoy. "I've never heard of anyone bearing your name before."

Lovejoy hitched her shoulder. "Ma named us girls all after the fruits of the Spirit. After me, she decided she'd best slow down and limit herself to one apiece, 'cept she skipped over longsuffering because 'twas a vicious mean handle to slap on a dab of a babe."

"You have a sister named Gentleness?" Alisa couldn't mask her surprise.

"Yes'm," Temperance answered. "Call her Nessie. Goodness — well, since we couldn't right well have us two Nessies, we call her Goody."

"Peace died of the whooping cough," Eunice said.

Chiming right in, Lois said, "And then their Ma skipped over using Meekness and gave Tempy her name 'cuz she was a-prayin' her man would stop brewing moonshine."

The room suddenly went silent. Ginny coughed, Daniel patted her on the back, then Tempy acted as if nothing had been said amiss. "Lovejoy's a healer back home. If comfort were one of the fruits of the spirit, Mama should have given that name to Lovejoy."

Dan didn't care much about the conversation. He had other things on his mind, but from what he saw, Comfort would have been an apt name for the young widow sitting beside him. She'd been soothing Polly from the minute she arrived. Once he shoveled in his own meal and managed to get Ginny Mae to have a few slurps of soup, he begged off any further social obligation and took the girls back to their cabin.

"Ain't niver seen a place so extraordinary as this here ranch," Lois said as they got ready for bed.

"I'm liable to pinch myself black and blue," her sister said. "Do you imagine our beaux will have such a fine spread?"

"They haven't been here long enough." Tempy's voice sounded muffled as she squirmed into her flannel nightdress.

"It's not just what they have right now; you have to imagine what a place you'll be able to carve out with your men as your years unfold," Lovejoy said as she plaited her hair.

"I cain scarce believe this." Lois climbed into a bed and scooted over to make room for her sister. "Above-the-ground beds — and just two of us in each!"

"Cain you fathom it — this whole cabin is just for them two younger boys. They each got a bed to themselves." Eunice crept in by Lois and thumped the pillow. "I'm thinkin' we could match 'em up with Uncle Asa's girls."

"Hold your horses." Lovejoy looked at her three charges. "Nothing's for certain yet — not for any of you. 'Til I'm positive those MacPherson boys are good husband material, no one's hot footin' it to the altar. Worldly goods don't count for much when a woman's heart is achin' from being hitched to a bad 'un."

"Don't worry for me, Lovey." Tempy buttoned her gown. "Whilst you tended Mike's mama in her last days, I got to know him. A better man I'll never find. Not a doubt tarries in my mind 'bout him and me being happy together."

"We recollect Obadiah and Hezekiah from when they come to buy their hound." Lois yawned. "They stayed to supper."

"The hounds stayed, or the men?" Tempy teased.

They all laughed. Tempy gave Lovejoy a hug and whispered, "Don't worry, Sis. It won't be like you and Vern."

Lovejoy's breath caught. She gave her sister a big squeeze and pulled away. She didn't discuss her marriage. Ever. "Guess I'd best blow out the lantern. Say your prayers and sleep well."

Exhausted from travel and toting that trunk, the others fell asleep almost at once. Lovejoy couldn't — not after having heard Vern's name. The memory of the children he fathered with two other women haunted her even years after he'd died. *Lord above, when will his betrayal stop hurtin'?*

Before morning broke, Lovejoy slipped out of bed. She dressed and tucked a knife in her leather sheath before grabbing a gunnysack and shimmying out the door. Purply blue with a mere glimmer of fading moonlight, the sky held the moisture of dew and the squawks of scrappy jaybirds. She took a deep breath of crisp air then let it out and set to walking.

" 'Morning, Lord. Thou hast outdone Thyself here. Cain't say as I expected it. Home was beautiful, but here — well, it just seems more green than gritty."

She took out her knife and started to identify plants and harvest leaves, bark, and roots. Back inside that dandy little cabin, her healin' satchel held some of the things she used most often, but it would be wise to start Tempy off with a supply of her own. More important, those wee lassies in the cabin next door coughed during the night. They'd been on the fractious side at supper last evening, too. Might as well put together a few things for this household while she was at it.

She hoped and prayed the Chances were right about the MacPhersons. They all spoke well of the bachelors 'round the table last night. Why, if Obie, Hezzy, and Mike turned out half as favorable as they sounded, her charges were trading up to a far better life than they would have had back in Salt Lick Holler.

Fine folks, these Chances. They'd make for good neighbors. The three married brothers and their wives billed and cooed like turtle-doves when they didn't think a body was a-watching, and the two youngest lads were right cute saplings. Too bad about that widow man Daniel. He's got hisself two darlin' little daughters, but he's grouchier than an early-woke springtime bear.

Daniel tossed off the blanket and sat on the edge of his bed. His stomach growled. The last thing he wanted was to go to breakfast, because those women would be there. His brothers and their wives never expected him to make much conversation — especially first thing in the morning. Their uninvited guests wouldn't know better.

Those three young hillbilly women chattered nineteen to the dozen last night. At least Lovejoy Spencer hadn't bothered him much. Instead, she'd held Polly on her lap and gently coaxed her to get through supper. He'd done his best to stay civil through the meal, and he'd done fairly well to his way of thinking. Coming back to the house right after eating was supposed to be an escape. He didn't feel like getting trapped into conversation, and the girls needed to go to bed. Nonetheless, he'd heard the music from the house and known the bitter tang of loneliness.

Coughs sounded from his daughters' cabin. They were both out of sorts last night. He wouldn't be surprised if they caught colds. Taking them on over to Miriam and asking her for some elixir would be wise.

He stood, stretched, and yanked on his clothes. His first inclination was to pad over in his bare feet, but since he'd take the girls to the main house, he might as well lace on his boots. Both socks on and the first boot laced, he couldn't stand it anymore. His baby girls were starting to sound downright croupy. Dan opened the door to the "hallway" and felt a flare of relief that the doors existed. Normally, he left them wide open so he could hear the girls, but he'd shut them last night to keep the stove's precious heat from escaping.

Five quick, lopsided strides to the girls. Diddle, diddle dumplin', my son John . . . How did that go? He forgot what Polly said next, but "one shoe off and one shoe on" rang in his mind. She'd be tickled at seeing him like this. Might make her perk up.

Polly's clear, high voice carried through the door, "Ginny, put your hand on your mouth when you cough. Do it like this."

Dan grinned as he opened the door. Polly was a bossy little bit of goods, but she did a nice job of trying to teach her sister things. His smile faded immediately.

"What are you doing here?"

CHAPTER 3

Lovejoy Spencer stood by the dresser with clippings that amounted to half the forest piled all over the top of the oak piece. Swirling a pie tin over the glass chimney of a kerosene lantern, she said matter-of-factly, "Your lassies are a-barking. Figured they could use an elixir to soothe their throats and loosen up the phlegm."

"Miriam keeps medicaments at the main house."

"I imagine she does. Problem is, the few a body cain get from the mercantile that actually are healthful pack a far too powerful kick for wee ones. Most of 'em are worthless and are little more than likker."

She hadn't said a thing he could disagree with. As she spoke, she rotated her wrist in such a way as to keep the liquid in the pie pan whirlpooling. A surprisingly pleasant aroma emanated from the affair. Even so, that didn't prove that she had any idea of what she was doing.

"The wrong plant can cause harm. I don't want my daughters to —"

"Right you are. But I've had me plenty of training and experience. I'm a granny-woman. I don't mean to sound puffed up, but I do have a knack with yarbs and such."

Yarbs? That did it. Daniel decided he wasn't going to trust his precious children to this backwoods woman.

"Neither of them's runnin' a fever, so I didn't add in willow bark. You've got gracious plenty out there, but seein' as how it's bitter, I'm just as glad not to add it in."

Everyone knows willow bark works for fevers and tastes bitter. It's going to take far more than that to convince me —

"But God be praised, it bein' summer, elderberries are ripe. I clumb up and got a wee bit of honeycomb, and out in your verra own garden, I found a hip on your dog rose. Fancy that, will ya? Don't normally find them till autumn's on the way. God provides, I say. We'll have your girls feelin' tip-top by the time they sit down to breakfast."

"I'll have Miriam give them what they need."

Just then, Ginny Mae let out a brace of coughs.

Lovejoy looked down at her with compassion, but Daniel refused to let his heart soften. His babies' safety rated far above this strange woman's feelings. "Come here, Ginny."

She poked out her bottom lip. "I want juice."

To his surprise, Lovejoy petted Ginny's hair a single stroke then gave her a gentle nudge. "Honor your father. Obey him. He loves you."

He lifted Ginny and tried to ignore how Lovejoy blew out the lantern and put down the pie tin. Wordlessly, she swiped all the leaves, berries, and twigs into a burlap bag. He hadn't meant to hurt her feelings, but she shouldn't have stuck her nose in where she wasn't invited.

"Daddy, the lady fried Sissy's socks on the stove."

A flush of embarrassment heated his neck. He'd forgotten to wash that sock again last night. Here it was, clean, dry, and fresh smelling on his daughter's leg. Her little shoes were tied, and the girls' bed was made up smart as a one-buck hotel's with the blankets all snug, then the sheet folded fancylike to peep over the top with something on each pillow to finish the effect.

"We'd better get on over to breakfast." He snagged Polly as she scampered past.

"I wanna take my mouse."

"Mouse?" He looked about. Vermin did manage to get in on occasion, but borrowing Delilah's Shortstack always worked. For being a little gimpy, that cat still knew her job and took it seriously.

"Miss Lovejoy made my mouse." Polly wiggled from his grasp. "See?" She pulled the little decoration off the pillow and galloped back over. A scrap of light brown cloth in her hand was knotted and twisted to form a creditable-looking mouse.

"I gots babies in a blanket, Daddy." Ginny pointed to the blue scrap on her pillow.

A draft swept across the room, then the door shut. Daniel stared at the far wall. Lovejoy Spencer had tried to do nice things for his girls, but he'd just put an end to that by rejecting her efforts. He didn't want her to be prying into his business or inviting herself.

Tryin' to do right ain't the same as doin' right. Widow Hendricks's words echoed in Lovejoy's mind as she stashed her gathering bag into the cabin. She'd wanted to help, but she'd overstepped. Daniel Chance was a good father, and he protected his daughters. Stumbling into a stranger first thing in the morning was good cause for him to be wary.

Too bad, though. The lassies needed something for their coughs.

Tempy lifted her head from the pillow. "You trying to beat the rooster on coaxing the sun up?"

"There's no time like dawn to take a bit of a walk. It's good for the soul to spend time appreciatin' what God made and gave. You gals hop to. Don't take too long sprucin' up, because these folks could be chasing me for the rooster's job." She left them and headed for the main house, sure she could lend a hand there.

Miriam answered her knock. "Good morning."

Before Lovejoy could respond, the door on the nearest cabin banged open. Delilah dashed out and around the corner.

"What was that all about?" Miriam wondered aloud.

"Don't rightly know." Lovejoy held a suspicion, but it wasn't for her to voice such a thing.

Miriam's brows furrowed. "I wonder. . . ." Her voice dropped to a mere whisper. "You'd be able to tell, wouldn't you? Eunice said you're a midwife."

Lovejoy avoided the topic. "Menfolk are gonna be hungry. I'm happy to holp make breakfast." She walked into the house, went

41

over to the stove, and stoked it. Her first order of business was to start two big pots of coffee while Miriam began to mix up a batch of biscuits.

Bryce toted in a big basket of eggs.

"Now looky there! You must have plenty of fine layin' hens to have so many eggs."

"Got us five dozen," he declared proudly.

"And he's named every last one," Logan tacked on as he brought in a brimming milk can. Daniel and the girls followed in right after him.

Lovejoy started cracking eggs into a big, green-striped earthenware bowl. "You men eat one egg or two at breakfast?"

"Four apiece, ma'am."

Shocked at his answer, she smashed the egg on the bowl's rim and felt the goo rush out over her fingers. "Four?"

"Well, the gals don't eat that much," Logan mused.

"Miriam?" Gideon sauntered out of the bedroom with a baby on his shoulder. "Caleb's got a rash."

Lovejoy wiped her hands on a dishcloth. "What kind of rash?"

"He's prone to diaper rash."

She tugged the baby from Gideon and cuddled him. "I'll be happy to scorch some flour. Got any zinc?"

"Zinc?"

"If we add it to the flour, it makes the rash heal faster." Titus scooted past Daniel and headed to a wooden box on top of the pie safe. "I don't know about zinc. I'm just hoping we've got Barne's Remedy in here."

"I have some in my satchel if you don't." Lovejoy held baby Caleb in one arm and started cracking more eggs. These men looked hungry, and Miriam was the only one here who seemed to have any idea as to what needed to be done to get a meal on the table. "Your belly givin' you fits?"

"Not mine. Alisa's."

"She oughtn't have Barne's. It's got rye malt. If the rye is harvested moist, it cain have ergot that'll put her into early labor. I'll make her soda biscuits and ginger tea."

Gideon poured himself a mug of coffee. "I wish we would have known that for Miriam."

Miriam nodded. "My first few months with Caleb were rough."

Tempy, Lois, and Eunice arrived. They jumped right in and helped set the table, make gravy, and scramble eggs. Freed up, Lovejoy got water to boiling for tea. She turned as Delilah came in. No one seemed to mind the gimpy, brown-spotted white kitten that dodged at her hem.

Lovejoy took one look at how pale Delilah was and suggested, "How 'bout you having a sit-down?"

"That's a good idea," Miriam chimed in as she led Delilah to a chair in the corner. "Lovejoy, why don't you bring Caleb over to her?"

Lovejoy caught Miriam's wink.

"I don't know what got into me," Delilah said vaguely as Lovejoy approached.

Lovejoy tucked Caleb into her arms and murmured under her breath, "Green as you are, I'd venture you got a baby into you."

Delilah gave her a flummoxed look. "I thought it must be something I ate."

"Alisa's belly's tipsy today, too." Miriam smiled at her sister-in-law and tacked on, "But everyone ate the same meal last night."

"No one else is sick," Delilah said. Her eyes widened, and her face flushed. She looked around the bustling room.

Miriam whispered, "Want to step outside with Lovejoy for a minute? I'll keep the men busy in here."

Delilah nodded. As soon as they were on the front porch, she whispered, "I can scarce believe. . . . Could I ask you a few questions?"

"You go on ahead."

It wasn't but a few moments later that Delilah let out a weak laugh. "I'd better get out a needle and thread. Paul's going to pop every button off his shirt. We've only been married six weeks."

Paul exited the house and shut the door. Concern lined his face, and he wrapped his arm around his wife's shoulders. "You okay, sweetheart?"

Lovejoy swiped Caleb and walked back inside. Some moments were meant just for two. A quick glance as she shut the door showed Paul enveloping Delilah in a hug and smiling like a coon in a henhouse. *If Mike treats Tempy half this good, Lord, I'll be eternally thankful.*

During breakfast, Polly and Ginny Mae's coughs left Daniel frowning. The only thing Miriam had that the kids could safely take was horehound, and that hadn't helped one bit. Lovejoy knew the right stuff for Caleb's rash, had nixed letting Alisa use Barne's Remedy, and got both Alisa and Delilah's stomachs settled enough that neither gal looked quite so green.

"Those young'uns of yourn have a case of the barks, don't they?" one of the redheaded gals across the table asked.

"Lovejoy's good with yarbs and such," the other redhead said. "She could fix you up

45

right quick with something."

One last look at Polly made his resolve crumble. Daniel cleared his throat. "Mrs. Spencer brewed something for them earlier, but it was too hot."

"It smelled pretty." Polly's eyes lit up at the realization that she might get some.

"Would you mind if I fetched it now?" Lovejoy asked the question without the smallest hint of gloating.

Daniel nodded.

A few minutes later she reappeared with a pale pinkish liquid in the bottom of a canning jar. Each girl drank her share, then the healer reached into the pocket of her apron and handed Daniel a tube.

He broke out in a cold sweat. "Nitroglycerin?"

CHAPTER 4

"No need to get riled. It's the cough elixir. That there's enough for each of your lassies to have another dose."

"This glass vial —"

"Oh, they don't use 'em for the nitroglycerin anymore. Onc't that man invented his dynomite, the mine stopped using blast juice. Asa Pleasant back home said he knew a company that had a heap of these glass tubes. He got me two crates, and they're right useful."

"You emptied them?" Titus asked the question, but he'd stolen the words out of Daniel's mouth.

She looked at him like he'd taken leave of his senses. "They wasn't never used. I got 'em afore they ever held a drop of anything."

Miriam patted Lovejoy's arm. "You'll have to forgive them. The Chance men are protective."

"Ma'am, seems to me you're blessed as

47

cain be to have such a fine passel of men as kin."

"Speaking of kin . . ." Paul covered Delilah's hand. "We suspect the family's due to see another addition."

"Already?" Bryce blurted out.

Daniel left the table and headed straight for the barn. Five years ago he and Hannah had made that announcement. It had been one of the best days of his life. The day they'd revealed they'd be blessed with a second child was just as sweet. *What kind of brother am I? Paul's thrilled, and I'm slinking away, licking my wounds.* But it hurt — seeing the wedded bliss his brothers enjoyed when he'd been robbed of his beloved wife.

Let them all celebrate. I'll hitch up the wagon and take those strange women to the MacPhersons. The horse snorted, and Daniel let out a rueful laugh. "Just what I was thinking."

As neighbors went, the MacPhersons were solid men. Honest. Hardworking. But odd! The hillbilly gals back in the house would be good matches for them.

It took little time to hitch the buckboard and lead the horse out to the yard. Daniel went to Bryce and Logan's cabin. They'd slept out in the barn last night so the women could have warm beds. Knowing he shouldn't barge in, he knocked. When no one answered, he tentatively pushed open the door.

The compact cabin hadn't looked this tidy since Logan and Bryce first moved in. Miriam, Alisa, and Delilah didn't brave it. Logan and Bryce set out their laundry on wash day and picked it up at the main house that evening. Bone tired as those backwoods women had been, they'd come in and swept the logs from roof to floor, dusted the surfaces, and made the beds. Instead of the normal jumble of items on the floor, his brothers' stray clothes, a harness, and the razor strop now hung neatly on hooks and pegs.

Daniel hefted the women's trunk, carried it out, and dropped it onto the buckboard with a satisfying thump. Satchels and a valise went on his next trip. Wanting to be sure he'd gotten everything they brought, Daniel went back to check. He almost missed the gunnysack. It barely peeped out from beneath Bryce's bed. One quick tug, and the bulging sack Mrs. Spencer had when she'd been in his daughter's cabin slid right out. Fragrances rose from it — pine, flowers, leaves — almost like a bouquet.

Hannah loved flowers.

"Mr. Chance."

He wheeled around and stared at Lovejoy.

She smiled. "The peace out here's extry sweet after all the mornin' ruckus, ain't it? 'Tis a blessing to have a big, loving family, but the noise cain be a bit much. 'Tis my habit to rise up of a mornin' and have some time to myself."

He nodded. Odd how she seemed to share that quirk of his.

"I come to tell you, when you give the lasses the elixir, they need to drink more water."

"Fine. I'll see to it."

She didn't fill the momentary silence with inane chatter. Instead, she stepped forward to claim the gunnysack. He shook his head in a silent refusal. It wasn't heavy, but he wasn't about to have a woman carry something.

"Thankee for loading up the wagon. My charges are eager to go meet their intendeds."

Intendeds. The word seemed so ungainly. Awkward. Not that charges was any better. The word lilted off her tongue as if she were some old governess doting over toddlers instead of a vibrant young woman.

Her smile faltered. "It's been nigh unto a year since I seen the MacPhersons. They had plenty to commend them back then."

She hadn't posed him the question, but Daniel answered it the best he knew how. "They're good to my girls."

Those few words drained the tension out of her jaw and shoulders. She beamed at him. "No one could deny what wondrous fine daughters you got."

He hefted the gunnysack over his shoulder. "What do I owe you?"

Lovejoy shook her head. "Nary a thing. You and your kin put us up for the night and practically killed the fatted calf for those feasts."

"You exaggerate."

Lovejoy's steady gaze held his. "If'n your family always eats like that, mister, this must be the promised land."

He hadn't paid much attention to what they'd eaten. Then, too, he hadn't paid much attention to this woman. Last night had been dark, and this morning he'd been worried about his daughters. Daniel took a closer look at Lovejoy. Had she been gaunt, he'd have spotted it right off, but now that he studied her, little things took on new significance. Her high cheekbones were a tad too prominent, her dress a mite baggy. She had narrow shoulders and delicate wrists. What he'd taken for being a slightly built woman was really someone who'd known lean times. It bothered him to think she'd gone hungry.

"Could be your lassies were croupy from the night fog; but if'n they don't shake their cough, you let me know. I'll fix 'em up more of that elixir."

"Lovejoy!" someone called.

"Here!" She turned in the open doorway, and Daniel caught a glimpse of just how narrow her waist was. Women often cinched themselves in for vanity's sake, but he knew Lovejoy owed her shape to a shortage of food. He wanted to haul her back into the house and feed her a big platter of steak and eggs.

Oblivious to his consternation, she headed toward the buckboard. Delilah's kitten, Shortstack, crossed her path, and Lovejoy scooped her up and absently stroked her. "Just look how blessed we are, girls. Mr. Chance hitched his wagon and loaded our goods so's you cain go see your grooms."

"Daddy, I wanna go see brooms, too."

He fought back his scowl. "No, Ginny."

"She's not coughing anymore," one of the redheads said. "Lovejoy's elixir worked in a trice."

"Mayhap you cain come callin' after we've settled in," Lovejoy said. She leaned down and tapped Ginny Mae's nose. "But for

52

today, best you listen to your pa and stay put. Here. This little kitty's a-wantin' a sweet lass like you to pet her."

Twice now Lovejoy had reinforced his authority. For all her strange ways, she had a level head on her shoulders. Odd as she was, he admitted she displayed a pleasant blend of kindness and common sense. *Another man,* he told himself, *might find her likable.*

Eager to meet the MacPhersons, the women scrambled into the buckboard without a bit of help. With his brothers there, it would have been natural enough for the women to be assisted. *They're barely civilized,* Daniel thought.

Daniel drove toward the MacPherson ranch, not knowing what lay ahead. He and his brothers had been on their spread for nine years; the MacPhersons had arrived in the dead of winter just this year. From experience he knew it took about five years to firmly establish a spread. Sven Gilder had tried to make a go of that sector and failed after two years, so the MacPhersons didn't need a barn raising. They'd shown up, gotten the land, and tended their own business.

Sven slept in his barn. Are the MacPherson men doing the same? We offered to help them knock together a cabin, and they refused. Daniel tried to ignore the mail-order brides' excited chatter. *Maybe the MacPhersons would have a tent. Plenty of folks lived in a tent for a year or so. Even with it being summer, these scrawny women'll freeze at night.*

Fencing. Every rancher worth his salt kept his fences in good repair. From the looks of things, the MacPhersons were doing a fair job of that. No cattle in sight yet, but they might be in a different pasture. Ground here would sustain a sizable herd.

"I wondered if the plants would be different from back home," Lovejoy said from beside him. "Plenty of what I'm spying is familiar."

Daniel shrugged.

"Rich soil. Looky there at how much it supports. The garden your womenfolk tend near burst through the fence, it was so bountiful. Do the MacPhersons have much of a garden put in?"

He shrugged again. Daniel had more than enough to tend without sticking his nose in on other men's business. The MacPhersons showed up for worship and lent a hand to others. They'd not been here but a week before they picked up the bad habit many other men in the region displayed of "dropping by" at mealtime.

54

"We brung seeds, didn't we, Lois?"

"Gracious plenty. We'll set to gardening straight off, Eunice. I reckon with this much property, the men ain't had much time to plant beans and such."

Daniel followed a bend in the road and sucked in a sharp breath. Lovejoy did the same.

His stomach lurched. He'd hoped things would be better than this.

"Lord be praised." The words spilled out of Lovejoy.

"That barn's twice as big as the Peasleys'." Tempy's voice held nothing short of awe.

Eunice started laughing like a loon. "Good thing I filled the trunk with all my stuff. Look at the house!"

"Yoo-hoo! Anybody ta home?" Lois cupped her hands over her mouth and repeated, "Yoo-hoo!"

A cabin just like the one they'd slept in last night sat not far from the barn. Lovejoy nodded approvingly. "Square-built."

"It's got glass winders," Eunice squealed.

"Whoa." Daniel halted the buckboard as Mike MacPherson came out of the house. "These women belong to you?"

Mike let out a hoot and dashed toward the wagon. "They're here!"

Tempy half-dove into his arms. He swung her 'round and 'round, and Lovejoy hoped with all her heart her sister had fallen into the keeping of the man God wanted for her.

"Temperance Spencer," Mike declared as he set her on her feet, "you are a sight for sore eyes!"

"Temperance Linden," she corrected. "Lovejoy's a widow woman."

He hugged her again. "Soon as I get the parson, it'll be Temperance MacPherson."

Daniel had hopped out of the buckboard and swept Lovejoy down to earth. "Thankee," she stammered. She couldn't recall anyone helping her in or out of anything — ever.

Ignoring her, he pivoted and assisted Eunice and Lois out of the wagon. "I have their belongings here."

Mike pulled away from Temperance. An unrepentant grin split his face. "We'll tote them inside."

Lovejoy held up a hand. "Hold it there. These gals move in; you MacPherson bucks move out."

"Wouldn't have it otherwise." Mike grabbed the satchels and valise. "Y'all come on inside and make yourself to home."

The girls flocked around him and squealed delightedly as they stepped inside the cabin.

Lovejoy lagged back. She walked alongside Daniel, who toted the trunk as if it didn't weigh more than a fistful of cattails. "Thankee, Daniel Chance. We're grateful for all you done."

He grunted, entered the cabin, and plunked the trunk against a wall. Squinting as he straightened up, he judged, "Cabin's well-chinked."

"Where are —" Lois began.

"Obadiah and Hezekiah?" Eunice chimed in.

"Obie's in the far pasture. Hezzy took a mind to go a-huntin'. Come suppertime, they'll find their way back home."

Seeing the disappointment on the girls' faces, Lovejoy rubbed her hands together. "Now if that's not perfect, I don't know what is. You gals cain surprise your men with the best meal they've et in ages."

Lois burst into tears. "Oh my — a real stove!"

"I left my gatherin' bag back on your wagon," Lovejoy told Daniel when he headed toward the door. The man had a fair stride, but Lovejoy never minded stretching her legs for a brisk walk. She marched right alongside him toward the buckboard. "Isn't it wondrous?"

"What?"

"The MacPherson land. Soil's vital 'stead of worked to death." They came to a halt, and she finished her thought. "Lots of promise in these here acres."

Daniel stared just over her shoulder in silence, as if he needed to come to terms with something important.

She surveyed the property and smiled. "I reckon this place is just one stripe short of the rainbow."

Steady and smooth as could be, he cinched his hands around her waist, pulled her close, and lifted.

CHAPTER 5

"The missing stripe is on that skunk wad-dling up behind you."

As if his actions hadn't been enough to startle her, Daniel's words took Lovejoy by complete surprise. He carefully set her in the back of the buckboard and speedily joined her there.

"Poor little polecat. Must be a mama, wor-ryin' over her kit if she's out scroungin' food in the daytime." Lovejoy opened her gather-ing bag and pulled berries free from the twigs. By tossing the berries in an arc, she managed to coax the skunk into meander-ing in the other direction.

"Little?" Daniel gawked at her. "It was big as a barn cat!"

"Gotta admire a mama who loves her young'uns." She wiped her palm on her skirt and nodded to herself as she nimbly slipped off the back of the buckboard. "A papa, too. Clear as water, you hold your daughters dear. 'Member to let me know if'n they need more cough elixir, and thankee again for carryin' us all here."

Daniel tipped his hat, climbed from the bed of the buckboard onto the seat, and headed back toward home. If he stayed here talking to that crazy woman, she might start making sense.

Back home he halted the buckboard in the yard and went to the main house to check in on his girls. Dressed in the little gingham aprons Alisa had made them for Christmas, they were "helping" Miriam make corn bread. Miriam glanced up at him. "Lovejoy's medicine worked. I'll have to find out what she put in it." She lifted the bowl and let Polly scrape the last of the batter into the pan. "Bryce is in the barn. Something's wrong with Raven."

Satisfied his girls were fine, Daniel strode to the barn. Of all the Chance brothers, Bryce had a gift when it came to dealing with animals. Most often he'd take care of things without asking for help or an opinion. Raven was Titus's mare, though. He put plenty of store in that horse, and Dan decided to see if his help was needed.

Bryce sat in a corner of the stall wrapping one of the mare's forelegs. "She's started nodding up."

"I didn't notice her favoring her leg."

"Neither did Titus." Bryce shrugged. "Nodding up means a foreleg. When a horse nods down, it's a rear leg. I felt her, and she's got a hot spot. We caught it early, and I mudded her. She ought to fare well."

Daniel studied the sleek black mare. Bryce wasn't a braggart in the least. Daniel shifted his weight. "You've a way with animals. If you're of a mind, I'll bring up a family vote in favor of sending you to vet school."

Bryce shook his head. "It'd be a waste of money. I have the hands and the instinct, but I don't have the brains. I wouldn't mind apprenticing for a season to pick up more knowledge, but in the long run, I'm content where I am."

Late that night Daniel tugged the covers back over his precious little girls, walked through the "hallway" into his cabin, and sighed. Hannah's quilt topped his lonely bed. All around him life continued. His brothers had married and were having children. Lovejoy Spencer was undoubtedly playing matchmaker with her charges and the MacPhersons.

Bryce's words echoed back: *I'm content where I am.*

Well, I'm not. My little girls don't have a mother. Daniel wanted to grow old with

Hannah, but all he had was the gnawing emptiness left by her death. *God, how could You do this to me?*

Heavenly Father, thank Ye for all Thou hast done for me. Lovejoy tumbled into the pallet and snuggled beneath the quilt. Going to sleep wasn't easy. The day rated as being one of the most exciting of her life.

After Daniel left, she and the girls had set to work. They'd spruced up the cabin, weeded what little garden existed, planted a summer crop with the seeds they brought, and fixed supper.

"You gals may as well talk out loud 'stead of whisperin'," she said.

Eunice and Lois giggled guiltily. Lois said, "They couldn't tell us apart."

Tempy snorted, "You couldn't tell them apart, either."

"Well, we only saw them once when they come to buy a hound," Eunice said.

"And they'd only seen you that once," Lovejoy pointed out with a laugh.

"We didn't ask them to marry up, though," Eunice staunchly insisted.

"You've got a point there. I 'spect it'll take a few days for you to iron out who makes your heart sing."

"Oh, I don't need no time a-tall." Eunice

sighed. "Ain't no man in the world for me 'cept Obie. He's got the cutest smile, and he loved my squirrel stew."

Lovejoy and Tempy exchanged a look across the pillow they shared and burst out laughing. "That was Hezzy!"

"Yeah. Obie's the one who et five of my biscuits." Lois ruined the solid tone of her assertion by tacking on a tentative, "Right?" When everyone else started giggling again, she said plaintively, "Well, they're both big and have beards!"

"Yes, you're right," Lovejoy sang out. "But Hezzy has a mustache, and Obie doesn't."

"Coulda just said so and saved us all this trouble," Eunice grumbled.

Lovejoy didn't want the girls to go to bed embarrassed, so she decided to give them cause to feel better. "Cain you jist imagine the men out in the barn? They're probably tryin' to figure out how to tell Eunice and Lois apart."

"And they have it real tough." Tempy snorted with glee. "After all, neither of them have mustaches!"

Two days later Lovejoy stretched to pick a few more flowering stems. "Now take a look here, Tempy. Yarrow. 'Tis good for wounds. Widow Hendricks called it 'Nosebleed' 'cuz a few of these tiny leaves in your nose stop a bleed."

"Lovejoy, I'm sure this is important, but you're staying here for a while. There'll be time enough for me to learn it." Tempy gave her a pleading. "Can't we do this some other day? I wanted to go riding with Mike."

"I'm trying to keep the two of you apart," Lovejoy confessed. "I don't want you to mistake a spring fancy for enduring love. A bit of distance lets the heart be wise."

"I already traveled the distance, and my mind's made up."

Lovejoy rested her hands on her hips. "Let's suppose you're right. Jist for the sake of laying the whole feast out on the table, let's see what all you're dishin' up. I grant you and Mike are a right fair match when it comes to smarts. He's got a sound head on his shoulders, and the two of you'll throw off a passel of young'uns that're clever as raccoons."

"Then what's the holdup?"

"What's his favorite vegetable? Does he rise up early of a mornin' in a fine mood? When money's tight and you both need shoes, who's gonna stay in the old ones?"

"We can learn those things as time passes."

Lovejoy shook her head. "Once you speak your vows before the parson, it's a done deal. If you wake up a month or year later and decide that man with his head on the pillow beside you makes you want to pack your bag and run away, you cain't. You're stuck. Best to be sure the table's solid afore you put your cookin' on it."

"Lovey, you know I've never been one to leap 'lest I looked first —"

"And I aim to make sure you're not changin' that habit this time," Lovejoy interrupted. "Anybody cain put on a fine show for a few days. It's when time moves on and wears off the polish that you see what you got for every day."

"I met Mike back in Hawk's Fall. I saw how gentle he acted with his ma when she was dying. It near tore him up, watching her go, but he knelt at her side. His pa's getting cash money from the sons, and since Mike's the only one who can write, I know he's behind it. That's plenty enough for me."

"We've always been honest to the roots, Tempy. I don't want that a-changin' 'twixt us. Truth be told, I wouldn't have brung you out here if'n I didn't think God was pointin' this way."

"Then —"

"Now you simmer down and let me speak my piece." She gave her sister a stern look. "When you marry up, you don't jist git the man, you take on his kith and kin. Obie and Hezzy aren't the sharpest knives in the kitchen. They're bigger and stronger. If'n they've got tempers, 'tis best we determine that now."

"The two of them are as dangerous as Asa Pleasant's new kid goat." Tempy's eyes lit with humor. "And they eat just about as much!"

"Supposin' you tied the knot and had to sit down to supper with them three men. Could you put up with livin' in Eunice and Lois's apron pockets? There's but one cabin."

"I reckon Mike's seen the Chance spread and knows they give their brides a house of their own. He'd not want me to have less."

"You're doing a lot of plannin' and hopin' and wishin', Temperance Linden."

"I've also been doin' a fair bit of praying."

"Are you asking God's will, or are you too busy tellin' Him yourn?" Her sister blushed, and Lovejoy knew her question hit a tender spot. She didn't belabor the issue. Gathering more yarrow, she said, "Even if things are sunny 'twixt you and Mike, you cain't verra well get hitched so quick. Obie and Hezzy would start pressurin' Lois and Eunice, and the four of them ain't even sure who likes whom yet."

"At least they've decided who is who."

Lovejoy winked. "As Mama used to say, 'Wonders never cease!' "

Tempy picked up a sunny, young dandelion, blew the dust from it, then ate the flower. "The only reason I'm not fighting you about waiting to marry Mike is because once I wed, you'll go back home. I can't imagine you not being in hollering distance."

Her sister's words made Lovejoy's steps falter. She exhaled slowly. "They'll need me back home; you won't. 'Tis the way of things. When you was born, Mama gave you to me. God gives us folks to love, but He never promises how long we'll have 'em. You're a growed woman, Temperance. I love havin' you 'neath my wing, but you're starting to test your own wings. Time's comin' soon when you'll want to fly and have your own nest."

"I'll always have room in my nest for you, Sis. Just like I'll take on Mike's kin, he'll take on mine. You know you're welcome."

Lovejoy laced hands with her sister and walked along the meadow. " 'Member when we memorized that passage from Ecclesiastes? It's been running through my mind. 'To every thing there is a season, and a time to every purpose under the heaven. . . .' "

" 'A time to be born, and a time to die,' "
Tempy said. " 'A time to plant, and a time
to pluck up that which is planted.' " She
reached over with her other hand and
tugged at Lovejoy's gathering bag. "I think
that verse is for you. You catch babes and
dispatch the old'uns to heaven. You garden
and gather."

Lovejoy blinked back her tears. "Time's
a-comin', my baby sis. Time's a-comin' for
you to love and for me to leave and go home
to Salt Lick Holler. I know it in my heart.
So long as you're wed to a man who'll cherish you, I'll thank the Lord and leave you in
His hands."

"Whose? God's or Mike's?"

"Sweetheart, Mike has Jesus in his heart.
If he's in God's hands, and you're in Mike's,
then you'll be in God's keeping as well."

CHAPTER 6

With the weather being nice, folks of Reliable were showing up for church each Sunday, same as they had since Miriam arrived. Dragging benches out into the barnyard for the service didn't take much time. Daniel helped — not because he wanted to attend, but because Hannah would have wanted him to rear their daughters that way.

"What are the two of you fiddling with?" he called to Titus and Paul.

Titus must not have heard him because he kept whistling — until he banged his thumb with a hammer and let out a yelp.

Dan posed the question again. Paul picked up the hammer and pounded in a nail as he explained, "It's too hot out here for our wives. We're setting up a canopy."

"Could have told me," he grumbled. "My girls could use some shade so they don't freckle."

Logan overheard that comment and

hooted. "You're fretting over your daughters' ladylike complexions? Oh, brother. Just wait till —"

"Just you wait till you have daughters," Gideon interrupted.

Dan cleared his throat. "While we're at it, we probably ought to put up shade for the MacPhersons' brides."

"Actually . . ." Titus scowled at his banged-up thumb as he spoke. "I've been thinking we need to have a real church building."

"You thinking of saving souls," Dan asked, "or saving your fingers?"

"He might not have any fingers left if he helps build the church." Gideon chuckled.

"We could donate half an acre over where the road forks between here and the MacPhersons," Paul suggested. "In fact, if we made an announcement today at church, we could have one built so they'd be wed in a church."

Daniel scowled. "Forget that nonsense. If they're following through with that cocka-mamie plan Delilah cooked up and marrying those girls on a whim and a letter, they'll need houses, not a chapel."

"Delilah's plan was brilliant." Paul stopped hammering and looked mad enough to spit nails.

"The only reason you're saying that is because it kept them from courting her." Daniel stared straight back.

Tension crackled for a moment, then Paul grinned. "So you figured that out, did you?"

"Even Bryce figured it out," Logan said as he nudged a bench to rest parallel to the others.

"What're the conditions at their place?" Gideon folded his arms across his chest.

"Single cabin 'bout the size of Daniel's. Those men hammered a big, old bent serving spoon to the door as the handle." He winced at the memory. "Lovejoy shoved the men out to the barn. Those four gals are sleeping on pallets on the floor."

"So they do have spoons," Logan dead-panned. "Even if they don't know how to use them."

Daniel grimaced at the memory of Polly innocently suggesting the MacPhersons use silverware to eat when they'd slurped stew directly from their bowls. "Before we go off half-cocked and plan cabin raisings, let's see if the women are willing to stay there."

Miriam had come out to place the Bible on the table they used as a pulpit. "They'll stay. Obie, Hezzy, and Mike are good men, and they'll be protective and solid providers."

"That's dim praise. There should be more to marriage than feeling safe and full."

"Daniel, after you left the breakfast table the day they were here, Lois started crying when we offered her a second flapjack." Miriam's voice quavered. "To a woman who's lived in want, the promise of a home and a full stomach must sound like heaven."

"The promised land." He looked at his sister-in-law and cleared his throat. "Lovejoy said this place was like the promised land."

Conversation came to a halt as neighbors started to arrive for worship. It wasn't long before the MacPhersons arrived. Daniel stood rooted to the ground in utter amazement.

"Their hair — it's sandy-colored, not brown," Logan whispered.

The MacPherson brothers' clean hair was just part of the shock. The hillbilly women had come and done the impossible: The MacPhersons were duded up and looked downright decent. Freshly bathed, hair clean and trimmed, rowdy beards clipped and disciplined, and white shirts crisply ironed. A man could have himself a real belly laugh at the henpecked transformation if the MacPhersons weren't positively beaming with delight.

"Yoo-hoo! Miriam! Delilah!" Lovejoy

scrambled down from the wagon and hastened up. "Where's our Alisa? She still peaked?"

"She's inside braiding the girls' hair."

"And your lassies, Dan'l Chance — are they chipper?"

"Fair to middlin'." From the look in her eyes, she'd wanted an honest answer instead of a polite "just fine." Daniel surprised himself by continuing the conversation. "I've kept them sipping plenty of water like you suggested."

"Good. Good." She bobbed her head. "It takes young'uns time to shake a cough." Lovejoy tugged on his sleeve.

"What?"

She drew another of her nitroglycerin tubes from a pocket and handed it to him. "I fixed up a fresh batch of elixir last night. Thought you ought to have it on hand just in case they need it someday. Mike tells me you cain read jist fine, so I pasted a label on it."

He held the tube and nodded. "Obliged."

She flashed a bright smile at him. Then her eyes popped open wide. "Well, imagine that!"

"What?"

"Reba White brung a saloon gal to worship! I'll go on over and welcome her."

73

Daniel choked and held her back. "That's Reba's daughter, Priscilla. She came back from a fancy young ladies' academy gussied up like that."

"Oh my. Thangs are different here. Back home in Salt Lick Holler, rouge and false yeller curls like that — well, it don't matter. God looks on the heart." She waved and called out, "As I live and breathe, Reba White! How wonderful 'tis to see you again."

Daniel stood off to the side as folks got settled for the service. His brothers managed to slap together a decent sunshade for all the women. Just as the hymns started up, he walked the girls over to sit at the women's feet. Lois and Eunice promptly pulled his girls onto their laps.

The MacPhersons must have told them to bring their instruments, because Lovejoy played her dulcimer and Tempy accompanied on her mandolin. Titus played his guitar. All in all, it made for some of the best-sounding music they'd ever had.

Once Titus finished leading the hymns, Mike stood up and hollered, "Fellers, that pretty one in the green dress what just played the mandolin's mine. Y'all cain listen and look, but that's it, 'cuz she's spoken for."

"That ain't much of an introduction," Marv Wall called.

Mike nodded. "Her name's Temperance Linden for now, but she'll be Tempy MacPherson soon as I get the parson here."

Obie rose, patted Hezzy on the shoulder, and said, "Other two are ourn."

"Which two? There're three left," someone called.

"The purty ones." Hezzy boasted. "Lois and Eunice come from back in Salt Lick Holler to marry up with us."

Daniel's eyes narrowed as he sought Lovejoy's face. Hezzy meant to compliment the other two, but in his backhanded, clumsy way, he'd just announced Lovejoy was plain. Only Dan caught a glimpse of her face as she sat down and turned to swipe Ginny Mae from Lois — and Lovejoy didn't look the least bit put out. She was smilin' to beat the band.

Maybe she just hides her hurt.

That thought stopped him cold. He couldn't remember the last time he'd thought about someone else's feelings. Well, that didn't matter. The important thing was, this conversation shouldn't disintegrate further and cause Lovejoy any more upset, so he stood and announced, "These gals deserve homes of their own. How's midweek

75

looking for you men?"

"If'n Hezzy didn't already have claim of me, I'd marry up with Daniel Chance at the drop of a hat," Eunice claimed as they rode back home. "Imagine him a-standin' there, rustlin' up holp for us to have cabins!"

Lovejoy gave Hezzy a piercing look. "So you've proposed?"

"Yes'm, I shore 'nuff did. Whilst Eunice helped me hitch up the wagon this mornin', I told her I was ready to get hitched myself. Eunice and me — we'll step together right fine."

As proposals went, it wasn't the most romantic thing Lovejoy had ever heard. Then again it was much better than Vern Spencer's shoving sugar and a length of copper tubing at Pa, then yanking her by the wrist and declaring, "Yore mine now."

Tempy nestled closer to Mike. "My man took me out to look at the North Star last night. Said he'd be constant as that star if I'd but wed him."

Her sister had already shared that sweet news with her, but Lovejoy knew Eunice and Lois were hearing it for the first time. Mike shot her a grin. He'd sought Lovejoy's permission for that walk, and he was prouder than a rooster with two tails.

"Don't you go looking to me to ask for your hand right now." Obie glared at Lois from the wagon seat. "A man's supposed to pick the time and place, and I'm not gonna have my plans all ruint."

As it turned out, Obie's plan unfolded at the lunch table when Lois found the ring she'd been mooning over at the mercantile. Obie managed to stick it in her mashed potatoes while Hezzy distracted her. "Reba tole me you liked that one the best."

Lois wound her arms around Obie. "I like you the best!"

"Hold yer horses there." Lovejoy set the bowl of peas down on the table with a loud thump. Several jumped out and rolled across the warped surface. "When we set out on this venture, I had a firm understanding — no weddings till I was satisfied the matches would last a lifetime. The sap might be running, but that's something y'all are gonna have to suffer. I don't want no spoonin' or sparkin' betwixt you. These boys cleaned up right fine and boast plenty of fertile ground and a decent herd." The girls all nodded emphatically. Lovejoy turned to the men. "These gals are hardworking, decent, God-fearin' women. There'll be years and years ahead for them to be your wives and bear your young'uns."

"Yeah, but —"

"No yabbuts." Lovejoy gave Hezzy a withering look. "A woman makes for a better wife if she's got memories stored up of how her man courted her. On cold nights when the babes are sick and the money's tight, a gal needs to harken back to her sweetheart days when her man promised her he'd stand by her side through thick and thin."

Lovejoy knocked her knuckles on the table. "I'm holding you all accountable. In six weeks, if'n you're all still moon-eyed, we'll have a dandy wedding. Till then, hand holdin' and maybe a kiss on the cheek's all yore 'lowed. Plenty wants doin' 'round here that'll keep you busy. You men, I want you fillin' the smokehouse."

"What smokehouse?" Obie muttered.

"The one we're going to build," Mike promptly said.

Lovejoy nodded. "That's the spirit. Onc't the new cabins are up, these gals are each gonna take one and get finicky as any broody hen does on her first nest. Gonna fix up a home you men'll each be proud to own."

"I'm already proud of this'un." Hezzy's brows furrowed as he licked honey off his knife.

"Rightly so," Tempy said. She looked at Mike. "Are Hezzy and Eunice keepin' this one, or do you reckon on buildin' three new ones so this'll be the extry one what serves as the family kitchen?"

"I get a new cabin, don't I, Hezzy?"

Hezzy wore the look of a man going under for the third time. "If that's what you want, Eunice."

Eunice beamed at him.

Lovejoy clapped her hands. "Now looky there. That's what I'm a-talkin' 'bout. Hezzy, years from now, Eunice is gonna recollect the time you promised her a home of her verra own."

Hezzy looked doubtful. "For true?"

"Oh, yes." Eunice gave him a starry-eyed smile. "I stitched a sampler with mornin' glories and made the purdiest geese in flight quilt you ever seen. I brung everything I could. We'll have us the grandest house of anyone in Reliable."

Tempy glanced at Mike then shamefacedly dipped her head. "I only had a few things to tote along here. Mostly, I'll fill our home with love."

"Darlin', that's all your man wants or needs."

Lovejoy took a serving of peas and relaxed a little. *Lord, things are turnin' out better than*

79

I dared hope. Please let this all work out.

Mike turned to his brothers. "What say I take Tempy and go to town tomorrow? We'll buy up the glass for everyone to get windows for their cabins."

"Glass winders?" Eunice squealed.

"We need to bring down more trees," Hezzy decided. "Pick up another saw, will ya?"

"Sure. Since we're havin' neighbors by, we'll need to stock up on vittles." Mike nodded toward the door. The men got up, walked out, yammered in a knot for a few minutes, then came back in. Mike looked at Tempy. "Best we make a list of what we need after supper."

"We cain make do with what's on hand," Lois said.

"Shore cain." Eunice nodded. "I'm a fair hand at tyin' lairs for hares and such, and you got beans aplenty."

"I'll go gathering with my sister." Tempy patted her. "Lovejoy knows what's good to eat, and we'll have greens —"

"I cain't do it," Obie said mournfully as he looked at his brothers. "I jist cain't."

CHAPTER 7

Hezzy's face went red, and he started chewing on his lip.

Lovejoy felt a bolt of panic. Everything had been going so well. Too well. If the men were going to back out, now was the time. But Lois looked ready to keel over from shock.

Hezzy shook his head. "I cain't do it, neither."

Eunice let out a wail.

"Wait! Wait! Eunice, I aim to marry up and give you that house. It's something else."

Obie snatched Lois's hand. "Same here, lambkins. I'd niver let you go. It's jist that we been keepin' a secret." He looked to Mike.

Any relief Lovejoy had felt over their immediate proclamations of love washed away at the sickening fact that they'd kept a secret. Vern's secrets never failed to tear her apart.

Mike shrugged. "I'm more than glad to tell 'em." He folded his hand over Tempy's. "We ain't rich, but we're far from havin' the wolf at the door. Halfway 'cross the country, we ran outta money. We worked at a mine."

"Mike knows all 'bout 'splosives. He made hisself good money — sorta." Obie's features twisted.

"The mine wasn't doing well. They couldn't make payroll, and men walked off. I was the only one left who knew blasting. The owner promised me a cut if I stayed on and we struck gold." Mike shrugged. "A week later, boom! We hit a real sweet vein."

"Gold?" Lois and Eunice gasped.

Tempy grabbed his wrist with her free hand. "Mike — you coulda got yourself blowed up!"

"Hezzy said the same thing. Soon as word got out that we made a strike, the other blasters came back."

Obie slid his arm around Lois. "We decided to take the money and get outta there. Came here."

"You didn't tell the girls because you didn't want brides who came for money," Lovejoy said quietly.

"Yes'm. We had us a pact not to tell 'em till after the parson tied the knot, but it's too hard seein' them fret." Obie squeezed Lois. "No brass or tin ring for my bride."

Mike cleared his throat. "We're not rich. Fact is, we spent most of what we had on this land and livestock." He lifted Tempy's hand and kissed the back of her fingers. "But you won't never go hungry or cold."

Lovejoy got up from the table, went outside, and walked down past the barn. There, in the shadows of the barn, she wept with relief.

"Kisses, Daddy."

Daniel scooped up his daughters and gave them each a loud smooch. "Be good for your aunts while I'm gone."

" 'Kay, Daddy," they said in unison.

"Take this with you." Alisa tucked one last dish into a crate on the dining table. "I really do wish we were going along."

"Absolutely not," Titus said from across the room.

"I could go," Miriam volunteered once again.

Daniel glowered at her. "Your hands are full enough. You're watching my girls, and Delilah's too sick of a morning to lift her head off her pillow."

"I need you to keep Alisa from overexerting," Titus added.

"And no one but you can feed Caleb," Gideon finished as he handed her their infant.

"You men planned that. I can tell!"

"Auntie Miri-Em, are they being Chance men again?" Polly asked.

"Yes, we are." Daniel set the girls down. "And you are to be Chance girls. That means you're to be nice to each other and obey your aunts."

"You 'ready told us to be good," Ginny Mae said.

"Daddy, you going to see Miss Lovejoy?"

"I'll be busy building. I'm not visiting with the women."

"My mouse got untied." Polly fished the scrap of material from her pocket. "Will you ask her to make it again?"

"I'll try to remember." He tucked it in his pocket and forgot all about it when they reached the MacPherson ranch and started building the cabins.

Plenty of men showed up to help, just as they had on the day Chance Ranch built cabins. Coming here and helping out was part of paying back a debt. It wasn't his debt — he hadn't wanted Miriam to stay on Chance Ranch and didn't help with the construction. Then again, the MacPhersons hadn't lived in Reliable at the time, so they hadn't helped, either. That didn't much matter, though. Folks here banded together. Lent a helping hand. Favors were bartered, and every last man here knew if he needed assistance, folks would turn out for him.

The MacPhersons hadn't anticipated building three more cabins this soon, so their supply of logs would be insufficient. Logan and Bryce had both gone over the past three days to help fell trees. They'd reported that other men had also shown up to do the same. By the time the work teams showed up on Thursday, they had enough logs to build two.

"Gonna need us more timber," Hezzy commented as everyone gathered to discuss the plan.

"We're nigh unto tripping over each other." Daniel scanned the crowd. Word had spread that there were several unmarried women at the MacPhersons'. Plenty of the men in the area figured that until the happy couples found their way to the altar, an opportunity still existed to get a woman to change her heart and mind. A handful of those men were already making pests of themselves.

"Todd Dorsey. Aaron Greene. Hookman." Daniel rapped their names out. "Marv Wall and Garcia — you men, too. Let's let these scrawny men build the cabins. We'll apply ourselves to downing more timber."

"You callin' me scrawny?" Obie's eyes narrowed.

Logan cackled. "I'd call you love struck."

Things were well under way by noontime. Obie let out a shrill whistle then hollered, "Grub's up!"

Gideon went through the line and filled his plate. Lovejoy smiled at him. "It shore was kindly of yore missus to let us borry her plates. Don't rightly know what we woulda done."

"You put out a fine spread. Men would have stood at the table and eaten with their hands." Gideon chuckled and snagged the last biscuit.

Lovejoy called, "Eunice, get t'other basket of buns. These men need plenty of vittles to keep a-buildin' your place." Giving Daniel a steady look, she lowered her voice. "That was a right fine thing you done today. Mostly, these men're fine bucks, but a couple . . ." She shook her head. "They was a givin' me fits."

"Lonely men do foolish things." He grabbed a biscuit from the new basket and strode off.

By the end of the day, three new cabins stood on the MacPherson ranch. Men straggled away, but Dan stayed behind. "Reckon yore here to claim the dishes," Eunice or Lois said. He hadn't yet figured out a way to tell them apart.

He nodded.

"Lovejoy and Tempy are packin' 'em up in the old cabin."

Daniel went to the door of the "old" cabin and stood in the doorway like a slack-jawed wantwit. He'd already seen the extensive gardening the women had accomplished in one slim week. This cabin showed a level of industry he couldn't fathom. Leaves, flowers, roots, and small bags hung from the roof. A bowl on the table held an arrangement of grapes, oranges, and cinnamon sticks. A wreath of drying flowers dangled from the buck's antlers over the fireplace.

"Take a seat." Tempy waved toward a chair. "We'll be done with the dishes in a trice."

Daniel watched Lovejoy tuck a dish towel between a pair of plates and remembered Polly's request. He yanked the scrap of material from his pocket. "When you're finished, could you please make a mouse for Polly again?"

" 'Course I will. Want me to show you how?"

Daniel shook his head. He'd already tried,

though he'd never confess it to a soul. Bitsy things like that never worked right for a man with big hands.

"Bryce said the lassies lost their cough and are right as rain." Lovejoy looked up at him and smiled when he nodded, then she went back to handling the plates with uncommon care. "Never seen me such pretty dishes. China, they are, delicate as a bird egg, but all a-matched up. You Chance men take mighty fine care o' yer women."

"I counted. Forty-five plates." Tempy handed the last one to her sister.

Daniel's gaze went from Lovejoy's hands to a shelf just over her shoulder that held a jumble of wooden, pewter, and glass dishware. He looked back at the blue willow plate Lovejoy dried so carefully. "Two dozen were my mother's. Alisa inherited the other half. They're a mite different, but the same company made them and the color's the same."

"Staffordshire," Lovejoy read from the bottom of the plate in a reverent voice. "Please give your women our thanks for sharing their finery." After packing it in with the others, she smiled up at him. "Now how 'bout I make you a mouse?"

The light brown square looked much bigger in her hands than it did in his. In a mind-boggling series of intricate folds, tucks, flips, and knots, it became Polly's mouse again. "You cain make this little feller move and jump if you hold him jist so and do this." She demonstrated cradling him in her hand and coordinating a stroke and carefully timed squeeze. Sure enough, the mouse wiggled and flipped.

He grinned at the sight.

"Dan, you ready to push off?" Paul was leaning against the doorjamb.

"Paul Chance!" Lovejoy called over to him. "How's Delilah's belly?"

Delilah's belly? Daniel nearly choked at her coarse question.

"She's sick as can be morning, noon, and night." Paul's mouth tightened with worry. "Have any suggestions?"

"That poor gal. She sippin' ginger tea like I tole her to?"

"Yes." Paul's shoulders slumped.

"She keepin' anything down a-tall?"

"Not much."

Lovejoy crossed the cabin and picked up a forked stick. She used it to hook the strings on a small muslin bag hanging from the ceiling. "I'll mix up some tea. Y'all have any melons?"

"Yes." Paul and Daniel exchanged puzzled looks.

"Real problem is her growin' parched. Boil a teaspoon of this till the brew turns the same color as this here leaf I'm putting in the jar. I want her to have a cup of tea laced with honey every other hour. Try her eatin' melon. It's mostly juice, but it might sit in her belly better than the tea. Tell her I'll be holdin' her up to Jesus, and you come git me if'n she don't start keeping more down."

Paul accepted the half-pint jar she'd put in his hands.

Daniel hefted the crate of dishes and made sure the little cloth mouse peeping out of the edge wouldn't fall out. Polly would be delighted to have that simple toy again. "Let's go."

"Y'all ride safe. Afore ye go, I wanna say I niver seen a man wield an ax like you did this day, Dan'l Chance. Them trees left standin' out there are prob'ly gonna start a-shuddering in fear when you ride past."

At first her praise sat nice, but as Daniel rode home, he changed his mind. That little widow had plenty to say, but it was always good. Such compliments and flattery from a woman added up to only one thing — she aimed to nab herself a husband. Daniel determined then and there to keep his distance.

CHAPTER 8

"There, now. Such a grand girl you are," Lovejoy crooned to the sorrel mare Obie lent her for the day as she saddled her. The girls were busy hitching a pair of sturdy workhorses to the buckboard so they could all go to town.

Yesterday the men worked from can-see to can't to make up for the house buildin' day. The gals worked alongside their men as was fitting — taking care of the barn critters, mucking stalls, gardening, milking, collecting eggs. They'd dug right in and done more baking and laundry, too.

"We 'spected you'd be fixin' the houses today," Obie told them at supper.

"We picked the feed sacks we liked the best to make curtains," Lois said.

"Until you all speak your vows, these gals are gonna sleep in this cabin." Lovejoy set down the law. "You men cain decide if you want to all pile down together in one of them cabins or out in the barn. That way you'll all avoid temptation."

No one argued with her, and to her utter amazement, Mike said, "I paid White for potbelly stoves. He's only got one in stock, so he'll bring all three up soon as the others arrive."

As if that news hadn't been enough to stun them, Hezzy dug around in his pockets and dropped five double eagles on the table. "We ain't had time to make furniture and sech. Mike says yore gonna need stuff. This'll be our weddin' gift to you."

The three brides stared at the gleaming coins in shocked silence. One hundred dollars. Lovejoy doubted any of them had ever held more than two bits.

"Go on with you now," Obie said. "Lest you think we're rich, though, best you know that's 'bout the last of what we got."

Tempy shoved it back. "We got what we truly need. You keep that and send it to your pa through the comin' years."

Lois and Eunice held on to one another. Though their faces were pale as dandelion fluff, they both nodded. "Kin comes first."

Mike took Tempy's wrist and turned over her hand. One by one, he stacked the glittering twenty-dollar gold coins there. "When a man and woman marry up, they put each other first, above all. We got faith that the good Lord's going to provide. He's never failed us. Now you go spend smart, sweetheart."

Spend smart. The girls were up most of the night assessing what they'd brought and what the men already had on hand, then making a list. Lovejoy tried to stay out of their discussion. They were grown women, and they needed to be making their own decisions. Judging from the list Tempy carried in her pocket, they'd proven themselves worthy of that trust.

Lord, those gals are heading toward the altar. Their hearts and minds are set, and from all I see, the men are good 'uns. Don't let me be blinded by this wealth of supplies or smooth talkin'. If there's reason for any of these couples not to wed, I'm beggin' Thee, please drive them asunder right quick.

Daniel got a sinking feeling as he rode Cooper up to the MacPherson cabin. It didn't look like anyone was home. Asking for help went against his grain. He hated relying on anyone, but he had no choice.

By breakfast, he knew he couldn't ask Miriam to watch the girls. Their coughs had returned with a vengeance and turned into nasty colds. Miriam's baby was cranky and feverish, too. Paul said Delilah was so green around the gills, she could barely lift her head off her pillow, and Alisa wasn't weathering her pregnancy any better. The way she looked reminded Daniel of how bad his Hannah had gotten whilst carrying Ginny Mae. He finally admitted to himself that his plan to avoid the Widow Spencer wasn't going to work.

So he bit the bullet, came seeking help — and no one was home. *Maybe she and the brides-to-be were all chattering up a storm and didn't hear me.* Dish towels flapped in the breeze on the clothesline, but that was the only sound. He knocked, opened the door of the main cabin, and found it empty. *Not empty, vacant,* he corrected himself. Lovejoy's "yarbs" filled the place.

Faint singing made him shut the door and turn around. Sopranos were singing "Oh, how I love Jesus." With their accent, it sounded more like, "Oh, how Ah luuv Jaysus." This time the hillbilly accent brought relief. The women were in the stable — well, make that coming out of the stable.

Daniel noticed none of the gals on the seat of the buckboard was Lovejoy. He looked at Tempy. "Where's your sister?"

"I'm right here, Dan'l Chance." Lovejoy rode straight to him then skillfully nudged

94

her horse to sidestep so as not to have it splash in a puddle near his feet. Her smile faded. "What's a-wrong?"

"Is it Delilah?" Tempy asked.

"Yore little girls?" the other two asked in unison.

"Both, and Miriam's little Caleb's taken ague, and Alisa's just too puny. Can you come check on them?"

" 'Course I will. Lemme fetch my healin' satchel."

Not wanting to waste any time, he lifted her out of the saddle and set her to earth away from the mud. She scurried into the cabin and called over her shoulder, "Don't you worry yourself so hard, Dan'l. Ain't nobody bleedin' or dyin'."

As far as reassurances went, it was as odd as the woman who gave it, but it worked. Relief flooded him.

Accustomed to making sick calls, Lovejoy had everything down to an art. She always kept her satchel packed for emergencies. By simply tossing in her nightdress and other dress, she met her personal needs. Knowing the children had colds and the women were suffering maternal difficulty led her to grab specific packets, then she latched the valise. Normally she wore her knife, but she'd

95

planned to leave it at home for the trip to town. Binding the sheath to the side of her apron, she whispered a quick prayer, then slipped the knife into place. Valise and gathering sack in hand, she exited the cabin.

Daniel Chance hadn't stood around whilst she was in the cabin. Hardworking, helpful man that he was, he'd busied himself checking to be sure the team was properly hitched. Though somewhat amused that he thought they might not know how to hitch a team, Lovejoy was also touched by his kindness. Women in his family probably didn't know how to saddle or hitch up horses — they were all fine ladies.

"You gals go on ahead." She tilted her head toward the road. "You know what to do, and we need to get a wiggle on."

Daniel lifted her onto the dainty sorrel mare and took the canvas valise. Once he mounted up, Lovejoy kept her mare going at a lively canter right beside him. "I'm a-tellin' you, this land is surely wrought by God. Don't it just take yore breath away?"

"Fine land."

He didn't seem overly talkative, but Lovejoy figured he was worried. "I don't mean to boast, but I'm able to ride without followin' a path. If'n you got yourself a shortcut, we cain take it."

"You got lost following the road the first day you were here," he reminded her wryly.

"Now there's the truth. Onc't I've traveled a place, I cain find it again, though."

"Straight off, or after you've wandered awhile?"

Lovejoy laughed. "Now there's a poser." They rode a bit farther, then she pulled back on the reins. "Whoa."

"What're you stopping for?" Daniel scowled at her as she dismounted.

"I'll jist be a minute."

"We don't have time to waste. Didn't you hear me? Women and children are sick!"

"We'll have need of these." She didn't pay no nevermind to his grumpy ways — men ofttimes got that way when a loved one was ailin'. If anything, it did her heart good to meet a man who showed such devotion to the children and women in his life. It was an admirable trait. Lovejoy took out her knife and harvested rames of mustard and put them in her gathering sack. It took such little time to glean a fair supply, and mustard — even dried mustard — made effective poultices. Whatever she didn't use in the next day or so could be preserved.

Daniel growled under his breath, "You're liable to step on a snake out here."

"Nope. The horses are too calm." She

tucked her knife back in the sheath.

Vexed as he was, Daniel minded his strength and gently boosted her back into her saddle. "No more stops."

"Fair enough. I got what I need now." She patted his hand. "You got yourself five brothers, but I got myself five sisters. I know what it is to love and fret o'er family. I promise to look after 'em for you."

Lovejoy didn't bother to ask where everyone was when they reached Chance Ranch. She could hear the girls' coughs from the barnyard. "Hoo-oooo-eeyy. They's a-barkin' all right."

"It's not whooping cough, is it?" Worry tightened his features as he dismounted.

"Rest your mind. That ain't nothin' like the whoopin' cough." Lovejoy accepted her valise from him after he helped her down. "I aim to make poultices for the lassies. They'll reek to high heaven, and the smell's likely to send poor Delilah into spasms. Best I prepare them o'er in your cabin. We cain have Miriam bring her babe in there, too."

Some things could be done by rote. Dicing onions and mustard, frying them in lard, and fixing them into poultices was stinky, but Lovejoy did it automatically. The girls stumbled along on their own, and Daniel brought along the cradle as Miriam toted

Caleb into the girls' cabin. "Tuck 'em in and be shore they all have socks on their feet."

"I don't wanna eat that. It's yucky," Ginny Mae whined.

"You don't have to eat it," Lovejoy promised. "Now clamber into the bed with your sister. Dan'l, I want their heads up higher. How 'bout you go stuff a couple feed sacks with hay? Those'll be right fine extry pillows."

"I've got extra pillows."

"Don't aim to use 'em. The stink'll get a-holt of the feathers and won't turn loose. Oh, one more thing: I got a mind to put together a stock of essentials for this ranch. Keepin' the girls out of the stuff's important. What say I use that loft up there?"

"As long as you move the ladder afterward so they can't climb up."

Once Daniel stepped out, Lovejoy pointed her chin toward the chair. "Miriam, go have a seat. I venture your son ain't sucklin' none too good, what with his nose all stuffy."

"He's not, but I know he's hungry."

"Wipe his nose best you cain. I aim to have him catch a whiff of camphor. That'll holp."

A few minutes later, Miriam had a shawl

over her shoulder. "It's working. He's doing better."

The plasters worked, too. By suppertime both girls still coughed but were able to eat soup and a biscuit. Caleb wasn't as cranky, either. Miriam decided to take him back to her place. Daniel fetched himself a cup of coffee and brought back a mug for Lovejoy. She smiled her thanks.

"So are they cured?"

"Nope. We got the symptoms reined in. This'll play out another two, three days. Coughs like to stay 'round for 'bout a week all told. Gotta keep 'em sippin' warm drinks, breathin' steam from the teakettle, and lying 'round. Don't want it to sink into pneumony."

"You'll come back tomorrow?"

Lovejoy gave him an amused look. "I aim to stay here. If you'll keep an eye on the sprouts, I'll go see 'bout holpin' the mamas-to-be."

"But you can't stay here. This cabin and mine are connected."

"I'm a proper woman, and I 'spect yore a proper man. Decent folk ain't gonna imagine any horseplay, 'specially with sick young'uns at hand. Come bedtime, you'll kiss your daughters and go mind yore own business for the night, and I'll bolt yon door

100

that goes to yore place."

Booted out. She'd gone and done whatever she deemed necessary for Delilah and Alisa then had come back and booted him right out of the girls' cabin. Daniel sat on his bed and strained to hear if they needed him. All he heard were his daughters' coughs and the soothing murmurs of a mountain woman.

He didn't like this one bit.

Two minutes later he slammed his door and walked out through the yard to the door of the girls' cabin. He didn't want to go through the hallway. No skulking around for him, no sir. He was heading out there where every last man jack on the place could see and hear him so no one would misconstrue this as anything improper.

He raised his hand to knock, but before his knuckles made contact, the door opened.

Lovejoy let out a surprised squeak. "Is something a-wrong?"

"What's wrong is, those are my girls. I don't leave 'em with strangers. They need me."

"They need water." Lovejoy stuck the bucket she'd been holding into his hands and promptly shut the door again.

CHAPTER 9

Vexed that he hadn't gained entrance, yet equally irritated with himself for not having seen to such a basic need, Daniel stomped to the water pump. Water splashed over the brim and dampened his fingers. His temper cooled. If anything, this gave him an excuse to march straight back into the cabin.

The door opened. "Thankee, Dan'l." Lovejoy reached for the bucket.

He ignored her and brushed right past. Wordlessly, he topped off the pitcher on the washbasin and sloshed more water into the empty pot on the stove.

"That's kindly of you." Lovejoy shut the door but stood by it.

Daniel knew she wanted him to leave; he turned away, picked up a log, and opened the grate on the potbelly.

"I just added a log. The fire's fine."

"It'll grow cold soon." He prodded the log already in there to make space.

"When that time comes, I'll add to the fire. No use wastin' wood or makin' the cabin smoky."

Any other woman saying those words would be quibbling; Lovejoy said them so calmly and quietly, Daniel couldn't very well grouse.

"No use having a hardworkin' man chop more wood when the fire's already fine." She gestured toward his daughters. They'd slept through the whole exchange. "Peaceable as a pair of played-out kittens."

"They're coughing."

"Aye, they are. I'm not aimin' to stop all the coughin'. Best that they bring up what ails 'em 'stead of keeping down low in their lungs. You needn't fret, Dan'l. I'll keep a weather eye on your precious lasses."

"You're a stubborn little woman, aren't you?"

Lovejoy hitched one shoulder. "Reckon there's a heap of truth behind that. I wrastle the enemy called sickness. Gotta be just as hardheaded and dauntless as him. If'n you went to battle, you wouldn't want no one marchin' alongside you that would turn tail and run at the first skirmish. You come and got me to fight for your daughters. I ain't gonna flee jist 'cuz you suddenly ain't shore I cain stay awake on my watch."

"I'm not a man to ask others to fight my battles. They're my daughters."

"No one said contrary. Problem is, you're a-comin' to this battle unarmed. You ain't got the proper weapons for the enemy of illness. Like it or nay, your daughters need me. You fetched me; standing here all night argufying ain't doin' them a lick of good."

Her words carried a sting of truth. Daniel looked over at his precious babies. "They're sleeping fine now."

"That they are. I give 'em another hour or so; then they'll be needin' some elixir. 'Round 'bout the wee hours, they'll start barkin' regardless of what they already took. Onion and mustard poultices again then. The bitty one, she's got a raw edge to her cough. I reckon she'll need sommat to soothe her wee throat then. I'm fixin' to whip up some sage gargle for her. Come first light, they'll settle down and want to sleep; but afore I let 'em, I'll have to get a pint of apple cider mulled with yarbs into each of them."

"You sound mighty sure of yourself."

Lovejoy took her shawl off the peg closest to the door.

Daniel's heart lurched into his throat. *What kind of idiot am I? My girls need help —*

"I'm fixin' to check them dog roses Delilah planted to see if'n I cain spy another hip. They're a right fine thing to give these young'uns. Mild enough for Miriam's little man-child, too. I aim to go get what's needed. Best you take a few minutes here with your lassies and decide what you want to do. I cain't fight you and the sickness."

The door shut. She'd left, but with the implied promise that she'd return. Plain-spoken as she'd been, her voice never took on a bite. She kept a soft tone so the girls wouldn't be disturbed. Daniel stood over his daughters and fingered the sweet little twirly curls that invariably sneaked from their braids and framed their cherubic faces.

They need their mama so badly right now.

The door whispered open and shut. Love-joy's raggedy skirt swirled about her ankles as she set the latch. " 'Tis a wicked cold wind for a summer night."

"When it blasts from the ocean, that happens." He frowned as she went to the washstand and set down a single rose hip. "One? You only got one?"

Her head bobbed. "One's what God provided. 'Twould be a waste to get more, anyhow. Moon-gathered hips carry a moisture that causes them to mold. I took just what the young'uns require this night. To-morra I'll search about. If I spy more, I'll gather them, 'cuz they cain be stored away."

Thin shoulders rising and falling with a deep breath, Lovejoy said, "Whilst I was outside, I did some soul searching. Those be your lassies, and you've done a right fine job with them, Dan'l Chance. That's saying a mouthful, seein' as you do it on your lonesome. Cain't be easy on you or them. Cain't say as I blame you for frettin' 'bout leaving them in a stranger's care."

She tugged her shawl about herself more closely and continued. "Back home, folks know me. I earned their trust. To you I'm nothing more than a hillbilly woman with a sackful of leaves and twigs and a boastful mouth. What say I meet you halfway?"

"Halfway?" He couldn't fathom how perceptive she was.

"I'll brew up the elixir and make ready everything for the plasters now. Onc't I'm done, we'll give the girls a dose, and I'll stay out in the stable. When I judge it time for the plasters, I'll come in and fry 'em up for you."

"You're not staying in that stable!"

A sad smile lifted the corners of her mouth. "Dan'l, lotsa places in Kentuck got grand houses full of book-learned folks a-wearin' fine clothes. The holler ain't like that. Your stable's better built and likely warmer than any shack back in Salt Lick Holler. Won't bother me none."

"You can't do that. You can't sleep out there."

She started concocting her elixir. Amusement tinged her voice. "Sleepin' wasn't in my plans for tonight."

The door jiggled. "Lovejoy?"

"Miriam," Lovejoy murmured the name just loud enough to acknowledge her presence, yet calmly so as not to disturb Daniel's daughters. She'd wheeled around and gotten the door unlatched before Daniel made it around the girls' bed.

"He's sleeping, but that rattle in his chest —" Miriam's voice broke.

Gideon followed his wife in and wore an equally anguished expression.

"Let's have us a look-see."

Dan stood behind Miriam and Gideon as Lovejoy pulled what looked to be an old-fashioned powder horn from her satchel. "Now you jist hold that sweet little man-child 'gainst you. I aim to loosen his swaddling clothes and have me a listen." Lovejoy pressed the wide, open end of the horn to Caleb's tiny back and rested her ear to the opening of the horn. She moved it about to listen a few other places then straightened up.

"Well?" Gideon rasped.

"Mullein ought to do him right fine. I got me some leaves. Makin' the tea's the easy part. Think you cain get him to drink it if'n we put it in a salt shaker?"

Miriam clutched her son tightly. "We'll do anything."

"Gideon Chance, I'll be askin' you to fetch a rockin' chair for your wife. A quilt, too, on account it's gonna be a long night. Cain you do that?"

While Gideon went on that errand, Lovejoy found what she wanted in that satchel of hers. "Best I not fix things in the same pot. Dan'l, do you have a pot or kettle o'er in that cabin o' yourn?"

It wasn't long before Lovejoy had several things going on the potbelly stove. Though he'd seen women at a stove much of his life, Daniel hadn't watched one do it to end up with the collection she arranged in tubes, vials, cups, and a pie tin. The mullein tea stayed in a cup, but Lovejoy carefully measured a few teaspoons into an emptied saltshaker. Binding a handkerchief over the opening, she said, "No race to get this down your wee man-child. Let him nuzzle it down through the cloth."

Later, though the kids didn't seem much better or worse, Lovejoy fried up the plasters. Daniel's eyes burned — partly from the fumes of the onions, partly from the fact that weariness left his eyes grainy. When that treatment was finished, Lovejoy nudged his boot with her foot. "Them lasses are wantin' your warmth and comfort, Papa. Kick off them puddle stompers and shimmy betwixt 'em. If we keep their heads raised, their breathin' will stay eased."

Daniel didn't crawl beneath the blankets. With the fire going, the cabin felt like a giant oven. He lay atop the bed, and each of his daughters wiggled and squirmed until finally nestling into his side.

Lovejoy went to Miriam and held out her arms. Miriam kissed her son and handed him over. "What should we do next?"

"Drag the rocker to the far corner. I'll plop down a crate so's you cain put up yore feet. Time's come for you to grab a bit of shut-eye. We cain't have you takin' sick."

"I'm healthy as a horse."

Daniel absently rubbed his thumbs down his daughters' bumpy braids and listened to their raspy breaths while watching Lovejoy coax Miriam into wrapping up in a quilt for a rest. Daniel glanced away then looked back. By an odd twist in life, he and Gideon had ended up wedded to sisters. When Miriam arrived a little over a year ago, Dan mistook her for Hannah. Any similarity between them no longer registered. All he saw now was a frazzled, weary woman.

"Miriam." He cleared his throat. "Go on through the hallway to my bed. You'll sleep better there."

She rested her head against the pressboard back of the oak rocker. "Thank you, Daniel, but knowing Lovejoy's just a step away makes me feel Caleb will be safe. I wouldn't be able to close my eyes if she weren't here."

"You prob'ly didn't sleep none last night," Lovejoy said as she walked the floor with Caleb over her shoulder.

"No, I didn't." Miriam yawned.

Hannah never lost a night's sleep when Polly was sick. The thought stunned Daniel. His hands stilled. He'd been the one to hold their sick babe through the dark hours. But Hannah was frail. Ginny Mae let out a raspy sigh, and he tugged the blanket up closer. Unbidden, the thought slipped into his mind. *Polly was well past her first year before Ginny was conceived. In those months, when Polly sprouted a new tooth or had the croup, Hannah slept while I tended our girl.*

Lovejoy nuzzled Caleb's temple and hummed softly as she swirled her hand on his back.

She's doing more for another woman's baby than Hannah did for our own. Daniel shook his head. Never once had he said or thought an uncomplimentary thing about his dearly departed wife. It was just weariness and worry.

Lovejoy eased Caleb into the cradle and approached the bed. "We need to turn the gals. Gotta move 'em so's any water in the lungs cain't settle. Think we could turn them with their backs to you, or will they sleep better if they just swap sides?"

In the end he sat up and slipped Polly across to his left side while Lovejoy carried Ginny Mae around to his right. While Polly started to burrow into a new place, Lovejoy coaxed Ginny Mae to have a few sips of water, then popped her into place and efficiently tugged up the blankets. Daniel's arms curled protectively about his precious daughters, and Lovejoy nodded.

"Yore a good man, Dan'l Chance. Them girls don't know how lucky they are to have a daddy who holds 'em close in his arms and in his heart."

By the time morning broke, Daniel held the conviction that Lovejoy would tend his daughters with diligence and care. He'd dozed off and on, but each time he opened his eyes, Lovejoy was checking his girls, stoking the fire, cradling Caleb, or measuring out a dose of something.

Lovejoy pulled on her shawl, picked up her gunnysack, and strapped on her ridiculous-looking sheath.

"What do you think you're doing?" he asked in a hushed tone.

"Now that the sun's ready to rise, the wee ones will stay sounding fair to middlin'. Onc't we hit sunset, 'twill be like last night. I've a few things to gather and get done. I shouldn't be long a-tall."

I'll come along. I don't want you getting lost. . . . Daniel's words echoed in Lovejoy's mind as she let herself into the main house where Gideon and Miriam lived. From the time she'd been here before, Lovejoy knew everyone ate as one big family in this kitchen. She set coffee to boiling, started a broth, and searched in vain for grits.

"Mrs. Spencer? How's my son?"

She turned. "He's holdin' his own, Gideon Chance — which is more than I cain say for myself. Where do y'all hide the grits?"

He chuckled. "No one can stand them. One of us can see to making oatmeal. Don't trouble yourself."

"Them gals ain't lifting a hand to do work

for a few days till we get them straightened out. Your Miriam's sleepin' like the babe in her arms after a rough night. Fact is, she's comin' down with the sniffles, and I don't want her sharin' them with anyone. Alisa needs to rest, and it's been a coon's age since I seed me a gal half as green 'round the gills as Delilah."

"I didn't think the women ought to. The Chance men survived on their own cooking for a couple of years."

She located the oatmeal, started it, and put beans on to soak for a meal later on. "I'm fixin' to go gather me more yarbs. You shore you cain keep watch on the breakfast?"

"We'll manage the food — I just don't want you going out there alone. We've got snakes and poison oak."

"You Chances mollycoddle women. That strappin' brother of yourn already fussed over my plan to go gathering." She laughed and touched her sheath. "I got me my knife. I'll watch where I walk, and if'n a snake takes a mind to say howdy, he'll make a fine lunch."

Gideon gave her a stunned look.

"Oh, now don't you be a-tellin' me yore truly afeered of pizzen oak. Onliest things I touch or harvest are things I ken. Them nasty leaves o' three . . . well, I leave them be!"

The corner of his mouth kicked up. "Miriam learned that lesson the hard way. Just promise me you'll stay to the path and in sight of the homestead."

"Fair's fair." She nodded and left. Walking along the edge of the yard, she took note of a few places where she could show Miriam to gather a few essentials, but a spot of land by the vegetable garden had her aching to plant an herb garden.

'Mornin', Lord. I'm givin' Ye my thanks for them young'uns makin' it through the night. I could pert near feel the angels stirrin' the water on the stove, jist like they did in them healin' pools in that Bethesda place in the Bible. . . .

Hands busy collecting yarbs, she carried on her morning prayer time. Granny Hendricks back home taught her that praying whilst she gathered carried a special blessing — that a healer who listened and spoke to the Almighty would hear His voice, follow His leading, and pick the essentials for whatever ailments and accidents lay ahead.

She'd told Daniel it wouldn't take long, but the bounty of this landscape exceeded her wildest imaginings. It took no time whatsoever to fill her gunnysack. Since Daniel gave her permission to use that loft, she might as well lay by a good stock of yarbs. "Lord, I'm thinkin' on bethroot. Ain't seen me none hereabouts. What with two gals a-carryin' babes, I'd shore like to lay in a supply."

"I talk to myself, too."

Lovejoy let out a surprised yelp as she spun around. "Bryce Chance, I swan, you 'bout skeered the liver outta me!"

"Sorry." He scratched the back of his neck. "I aim to take that sorrel back to the MacPhersons' 'less you say otherwise."

"Now that's kind as cain be. I'm shore Obie has need of her."

Bryce took the gunnysack from her. "Dan said not to let you go far afield."

Lovejoy tried not to gape. "Dan'l sent you to hover over me like a guardian angel out here?"

"He said a stiff wind could blow you straight to Texas." He frowned as he looked at the bag in his hand. "This is too heavy for a dab of a woman."

"Your big brother worries too much." Though she said the words, something deep inside warmed at the thought that Daniel didn't just pay lip service to her safety — he'd needed to stay with his daughters, but he'd made sure his brother shadowed her.

"Can't blame Dan. Mama and Hannah are both buried yonder. We're all antsy 'bout womenfolk."

"Hannah was his wife?"

Bryce nodded curtly.

"I'm sorry. Did she pass on recently?"

"Nah. Little over two years past — right after Ginny Mae was born. Best you not talk of her. Dan's been half-crazy with grief."

They walked back to the barnyard in silence, and Bryce handed her the gathering sack at the pump, then headed toward the stable. Lovejoy paused at the pump, washed her hands free of the sap and dirt, and rinsed the blade of her knife. Stretching and looking about, she let out a sigh and whispered, "Dear Lord in heaven, look down on me. I'm a-needin' strength and wisdom. Plenty needs doin' 'round here, and my mind's whirlin' round foolish thoughts."

The foolish thoughts didn't go away. As the day progressed, Lovejoy reminded herself that she didn't ever want to marry again — not even if someone as stalwart as Daniel Chance asked. Besides, he wasn't asking, and folks back home relied on her. They needed a healer in Salt Lick Holler.

CHAPTER 10

"Red flannel?" Daniel echoed Lovejoy's request as soon as he took a gulp of oatmeal. Someone hadn't tended the pot, and the cereal tasted scorched.

It was the first time since Miriam had come that one of the brothers had made breakfast. Daniel hoped it was the last.

Logan made a face and dumped sugar in his bowl; Titus opted for drowning his in milk and salt. Paul plopped a blob of butter in his, but it was all in vain. No amount of doctoring would fix their breakfast.

Lovejoy took a bite and bobbed her head. "Yes, yes. Red flannel. Gideon, thankee for makin' the meal. It makes me warm clear through."

"Glad you like it." Gideon smiled, but Dan figured he had reason — he'd gotten a fair night's sleep.

Alisa suppressed a shudder and washed down the only bite she'd tried with some ginger tea. "I have some white flannel. You're welcome to it."

"That's powerful nice of you to offer, 'specially seein' as how you need that flannel to stitch baby gowns, but I'll turn it away." Lovejoy rose. A moment later she returned with a little bowl filled with berries and a cup of cream, which she set down in front of Alisa, effectively nudging away the oatmeal. She patted Alisa's arm. "Not often I'm picky, but this is one of them times. I'm wantin' red."

It's not like her to be so persnickety. Dan shook his head at how she sat down, took another bite, and swallowed without letting on just how foul the stuff tasted. If she could be satisfied with this, why couldn't she be satisfied with white flannel?

"Red makes the best poultices and plasters. Need lemons and lemon drops, too. Whichever of you bucks moseys into town, I'll be asking for them as well."

"Lemons?" Bryce echoed.

"Lemon drops?" Logan looked like he didn't know whether to be confused or thrilled at that order.

Calm as you please, Lovejoy took another spoonful of oatmeal, downed it, and confirmed, "Aye. I recollect seein' a whole bushel of lemons in Reba's mercantile. They smelled dreadful good."

"Get her whatever she wants," Paul muttered.

"It's for that bride o' yourn," Lovejoy said. "Lemonade or suckin' on them drops helps with the sickness."

Paul shot to his feet. "Why didn't you say so? We have horehound —"

"Lemon's the onliest candy that'll do."

Paul accepted that outrageous notion without batting an eye. "Fine. What else do you need?"

"That's it, unless they got a library."

"A library?" the Chance brothers asked in unison.

"I reckon I may as well learn me a bit 'bout the yarbs what grow in this place. Some stuff don't grow but in special places, and I have a hankering to take advantage of this opportunity. I'll collect a passel o' whatever's beneficial, leave some here, and take the rest back home when I go."

"You're not staying?" The words tumbled out of his mouth before Daniel could hold them back. That sleepless night was making him do stupid things.

"I aim to change your mind," Titus declared. "I want you around when Alisa needs a midwife."

"And when Delilah does, too!" Paul

slapped his hat on his head and glowered at Lovejoy. "I'm going to get red flannel, lemons, and lemon drops. One more thing: I'm going to see if White's Mercantile has a spare pair of handcuffs, because I'll do whatever I have to, to keep you here!"

Lovejoy merely laughed. Plainly, she didn't understand just how serious Paul was. *The man is besotted by his bride. Just like I was. . . .*

As his brothers divvied up the chores for the day, Daniel ignored their plans. He'd work in the barnyard, the stable — anything close to home. Whenever his girls were under the weather, that was a given.

"Dan'l." Lovejoy's voice jarred him out of his thoughts. He looked up from his barely touched oatmeal. "The young'uns are gonna give us fits again tonight. 'Member where the mustard was when you brung me? I'd take it kindly if'n you got a mind to gather a passel more on account of, by tomorrow, we'll use up all I cut."

"I know where there's some mustard," Alisa said. "I'll get it."

"Nope. Ain't gonna see you walking farther than the yard. Yore ankles done swoll up over the night. Most you oughtta be doin' is stitchin' and readin'."

Alisa blushed to the roots of her hair. Dan

couldn't be sure whether it was because she was trying to keep it a secret from Titus or if it was because Lovejoy spoke of such anatomy in mixed company.

Titus gave his wife a horrified look. "What's wrong? Why didn't you tell me —"

"I'm fine, I'm sure," Alisa murmured.

"Don't bother growin' gray o'er that, Titus," Lovejoy said. "Her hands ain't swoll a-tall. It's when a mama-to-be's hands and face get swoll up that you got cause to fret. I niver seen me men who clucked like hens over their women and kids like you Chance boys."

"They're very good men." Though Alisa included them all in her words, Dan noticed she kept her gaze trained on Titus.

Lovejoy chuckled. "Cute as a litter of speckled pups, if'n you ask me."

"I'll get the mustard on my way home," Paul said.

Alisa started to giggle. "Look for a few bones, too."

"You even chop vegetables purdy."

Alisa looked across the table at Lovejoy and laughed. "I do?"

"Looky there." Lovejoy gestured at the colorful heap. "You don't hack at 'em with your blade; you cut 'em all of like size. And you got it arranged in an arc about you like a rainbow with the stripes a-going up and out 'stead of side to side."

"I feel ridiculous sitting here while you're working."

Lovejoy took two pots and a kettle over to the table. "Beans in here," she said as she scooped half of the tomatoes into the larger pot then put the rest of the tomatoes and vegetables in the kettle. "You're doing plenty of important things, Alisa Chance. First off, you're carrying a new life. Ain't anything more important a woman cain do than that."

"Any woman can carry a child."

Lovejoy looked her in the eye and felt the waves of pain wash over her for an instant before she resigned them to the Almighty. "Not every woman, Alisa."

Dumping her last handful of beans into the pot, Alisa sucked in a sharp breath. "Oh, Lovejoy. I'm sorry. That was —"

"Now don't you start frettin'. I need you to be clear-thinkin' on account of I need to know what Delilah's been able to tolerate so's we cain perk up her appetite."

"Other than an occasional soda biscuit, she's not keeping much of anything down. I figured on making biscuits to go with the soup you're planning."

"That's a right fine idea. After you take a nap, I expect it'll be 'bout time for you to start in on that."

"Nap!" Alisa gave her an outraged look. "I'm not going to lie around while you work."

"Yup, you are." Lovejoy started stewing the tomatoes and said over her shoulder, "Never did see me any reason to beat 'round the bush, so here goes: The ox is in the ditch here. This is a big ranch with plenty that needs doin'. All three young'uns are ailin', and Miriam's hands are full with them today. You and Delilah best behave yourselves, else you're risking the lives you carry. 'Stead of frettin', why don't we praise Jesus that I'm strong and cain fill in?"

"Fill in? Lovejoy, you did laundry, too!"

"Day's fair and sun's strong. Good time to let the whites bleach on the line." She stirred sautéed onions into the tomatoes and added in broth and a sprinkling of mild spices. Last night's leftover rice finished the recipe. This would be for the children and women. The menfolk would be having a hearty Brunswick stew. "I ken 'tisn't Saturday night, but seems to me Delilah would feel a far sight better if we tubbed her. No use lettin' the hot water go to waste, so what say you have a soak? It'll loosen you up afore your nap."

"You're doing too much."

Lovejoy laughed. "One of these days when the shoe's on the other foot and my Tempy's in a fix with Lois and Eunice, you'll return the favor."

"You'll be there —"

"She said she would be leaving soon," Daniel said as he came in. He lifted his chin toward Lovejoy. "I put another pair of onions in the girls' cabin for tonight."

"Thankee, Dan'l."

He crossed the kitchen, lifted a spoon, and took a taste of the soup she'd started for the children. Humming appreciatively, he grabbed a mug, dunked it, and started drinking. He turned to Alisa. "You found Ma's recipe!"

"Who cares about a recipe! Daniel, she can't leave. We need her! I need her." Alisa started to cry.

Wincing, he gave his sister-in-law an awkward pat. "Now, Alisa . . ."

"Folks back home are expecting me," Lovejoy said in a level tone. She'd found sympathy usually made a maternity patient worse instead of calm. "Widow Hendricks is fillin' in as the healer, but it's temporary."

"But they'll have her. We don't have anyone." Alisa took hold of Daniel's sleeve.

124

"Tell her, Dan. Tell her how we need her to stay."

Daniel looked like he'd gladly give up his best horse to anyone who'd bail him out of this situation.

"Things have a way of working out. I've tended well o'er a hundred births, so I speak from experience. Why, look right under your nose. Miriam and Caleb seem to be just fine."

"But Dan's wife died." The words curled in Alisa's throat.

Lovejoy tilted her head and frowned. "Dan'l, is that the gospel truth?"

CHAPTER 11

Dan's wife died. Alisa's outburst shocked him. No one mentioned Hannah's passing. Ever. He wouldn't put up with it. As if that wasn't bad enough, Lovejoy expected him to talk about it.

"If'n a woman passes on in the first ten days, it's the childbearing. That's why I'm askin'."

He managed to mumble something about two months.

Lovejoy plopped down, disentangled him from Alisa's terrified grasp, and pulled the weeping woman into her arms. "See? You've been worryin' for naught. May as well have yourself a fine caterwaul. Cleanses the heart. Dan'l, we'll see you at supper."

He got out of there fast. Never once had it occurred to him that by keeping silent about Hannah, he'd given Alisa cause for worry. *Worry? Panic. Alisa was scared half out of her mind. Come to think on it, Paul went*

126

to fetch Delilah for Miriam so she'd have some support.

"Dan?" Miriam called to him from the girls' cabin. "I need to go get a few things. Would you mind staying with the kids?"

He paced to his cabin and frowned. "Sounds like you're catching what the kids have."

"No need to worry, Dan. I'll be fine. It's nothing much, and I have no doubt Lovejoy will concoct something to help me improve. I won't be but a minute; I need to fetch diapers for Caleb."

Dan thought about Alisa crying in Lovejoy's arms. "Diapers on the line ought to be dry by now."

Miriam smiled. "Lovejoy's mother should have named her Mercy. I declare, the woman has more compassion than anyone I've ever met."

Polly and Ginny Mae were growing restless at their dolly tea party and started dressing Shortstack in doll clothes. The kitten seemed remarkably tolerant of that indignity, so Daniel didn't put a stop to it. When Miriam returned with a stack of diapers, he left. Plenty of chores needed doing and kept his hands busy, but his mind stayed far busier.

He could say exactly — to the day — how

long Hannah had been gone. Two years, one month, and three days. Some days it felt like it was just yesterday; other moments he felt as if he'd lived a lifetime since then. Day by day he made it through for his daughters' sake. Today, though, reality smacked him in the face. Everyone else was still doing things for his sake — not tasks or favors, but shielding him as if he weren't man enough to deal with his sorrow.

And I haven't been.

The thought staggered him. Grief was normal. Even Jesus wept when He learned of Lazarus's death. The emptiness inside wouldn't change, but Dan determined not to cause others sorrow because of it.

Hearing Lovejoy say anything past ten days probably wasn't related to the birthing released him of a burden he'd been carrying for more than two years now. Reba White was gone when Hannah went into labor with Ginny Mae, and Dan had to deliver their child. When Hannah didn't spring back after the birthing, he'd worried he'd done something wrong. But Lovejoy said she'd tended over a hundred births. Surely she would know whereof she spoke.

I've been troubled by that for years. The relief is unspeakable. He cast a glance back toward the house. Scrawny little Lovejoy's plainspoken words had lifted a burden from his shoulders that he'd carried for far too long. With his guilt assuaged, the sorrow persisted . . . but it was almost bearable.

Alisa shouldn't have had to worry all these months. The least I can do is give her and Delilah peace of mind when it comes to them being in a motherly way. And I'm going to be certain Lovejoy stays to attend them when their time comes. She's got a merciful heart and a gentle touch. Add to that, she's capable. I'll do anything to safeguard my brothers' wives and make sure Titus and Paul never carry the burden I have.

In the distance, he watched Lovejoy and Delilah take the wash off the clothesline. Delilah seemed to have perked up a bit. Having Lovejoy here was a good idea. She'd managed to rescue them all from a bad situation. *I'll keep her here to be sure things go well.*

Having her here is a disaster. Daniel glowered at Lovejoy two mornings later. He'd slept in his cabin last night and come to check the girls this morning. One look, and he'd been livid. Fortunately, the girls were well enough to go to the main house for breakfast, so he'd sent them ahead. Now he blocked Lovejoy's exit. "What were you thinking?"

She hitched her shoulder in a careless manner. "Things that need doin', need doin'. I've got me a strong back and willing hands."

"It doesn't give you the right to meddle." He gestured wildly at the girls' cabin. Since last evening, she'd rearranged the furniture, moved the dollhouse, and set a little box down by the washstand so the girls could splash around on their own. Lovejoy hadn't stopped there. She'd twisted and tied twigs to form a heart, then stuck little flowers in it and hung it up over the bed while tacking one of Delilah's paintings up on another wall.

"It didn't need doin'; it was unnecessary."

"Draft blowing 'neath the door used to keep some of the heat from radiating to their bed." She waved toward the little table and chair set the brothers had made for his girls. "Sun hits that table cheerful-like. It'll be easier on their eyes onc't they start readin' and cipherin'."

"There's time yet before then. You can forget feathering this nest, because you're not going to roost here."

Lovejoy laughed outright. "Roost?"

"We do fine, my daughters and I. We don't need another woman in our lives, so you can just march back to the MacPhersons'. They're interested in brides; I'm not."

"You're daft as a drunken duck if you figure I ever want to wed again. I got no need to."

He crooked a brow in disbelief.

"Think on it. I got me a marketable skill and make a fair living on my own. Fact is, you fetched me for holp, and holp is what I'm a-givin'. Since we've cleared the air, you cain just get out of my way, because I don't aim to scoot off until I'm satisfied everyone at Chance Ranch is on the mend."

Daniel stared at her.

She stared straight back. Amusement sparkled in her eyes.

"You're laughing at me."

Her head bobbed. "That's a fact. If'n you come up with more of those crazy notions, I'll be in trouble. The yarb I use back home for pullin' a bent mind straight don't grow here."

"You're a pushy woman. I don't like pushy women."

"To my way of reckonin', Dan'l, you don't like most anybody. I seen you with your kin, and I seen you at Sunday worship. Onliest man I ever knew who scowled more'n you was Otis Nye from back home. He done lost both legs in the War 'twixt the States, and he spends all his time carvin' wood into the ugliest owls ever seen. Has his cousin put them up on the barn to scare folks away, but I never saw the reason. Ain't a soul who wants to pay visits to such a cantankerous coot."

"Are you calling me cantankerous?"

She sucked in one cheek and chewed on it a second as she studied him then nodded. "Yup." She dusted off her hands as if she'd just handled a gritty task. "Now you gonna move so's I cain go holp with breakfast?"

He stepped aside and watched her go toward the house. She paused at Delilah's flower garden, plucked a few flowers and leaves that she promptly tucked into her apron pocket, and disappeared into the house.

There's nothing wrong with me, and I'm not cantankerous. As he reached to shut the cabin door, he caught sight of himself in the just-rearranged washstand mirror. He was scowling.

"I've been five days gone, and I cain scarce believe this is the same place." Lovejoy turned and looked about the MacPherson spread.

"We've been busy." Tempy gave her a hug.

"Hezzy turned over more ground," Eunice said, "and we put in even more of a garden."

"And just wait till you see my cabin." Lois took on a dreamy look. "Aunt Silk would swoon if'n she got a gander at how fine it is."

Lovejoy laughed with delight. "It's a fine thing to hear all's goin' so well. So why don't you gals show me what you done in those cabins?"

"First off, we made sure to take care of the larder," Tempy said as she led her to the main cabin.

"Keep a man warm and fed, and he's happy," Eunice chimed in.

Lois giggled. "With them in the stable and us all in here, I don't think they're warm at all."

"And it's going to stay that way till you all speak your vows," Lovejoy said as she gave Lois a playful poke in the arm.

Tempy raced to the shelves in the cabin. "Look, Lovejoy. We got us nice dishes. We're going to set our men a fine table."

Lovejoy watched as the girls showed her what they'd gotten — flatware, mixing bowls, a generous supply of canning jars, and a sadiron. They'd laid in a wise selection of food, too. "My, you gals did yourselves proud."

"We prayed," Tempy said. "When you rode off with Daniel, we prayed for his kin, for our men, and to have wisdom so we'd be wise stewards and good wives."

"God surely answered your prayers."

"Can we show her the cabins now?" Lois could scarcely contain herself. "We ain't seen each others' yet. It just seemed like more fun to have a grand show."

"Let's look at yourn first." Lovejoy locked arms with her.

They went to Lois and Obie's. Lovejoy stood at the door in shock. "You got an above-the-ground bed!"

"Couldn't not," Eunice explained as she reverently ran her fingers over the carved oak headboard. "Miz White o'er at the mercantile, she made us a fine deal. Bed, dresser, and — she used a highfalutin name — 'commode' came to fifteen dollars a set. Even included a ticking."

"Tempy told us to add clover to the hay to keep 'em smelling sweet."

Lovejoy cast a smile at her sister.

Tempy pointed at the blankets atop the bed. "Good, thick, wool covers."

"And the pillow slips you brung look fancy as cain be," Lovejoy praised.

They went to Eunice and Hezzy's cabin next. Lois got excited at the sight of the tintype of their parents. Lovejoy admired the pitcher hanging from a peg. "The daffodils on that are enough to cheer up any mornin'."

"The washbowl's just plain white." Eunice didn't look the least bit sad. "Unmatched sets was half the price. Bought me my verra own hairbrush and comb. Lois cain keep the old ones."

Finally, they ended up in the cabin that would belong to Tempy and Mike. Seeing the first two should have prepared Lovejoy for the last, but it hadn't. She stepped into what would be Tempy's bridal bower, and tears flooded her eyes.

"Mama's crown-of-thorns quilt!"

Tempy snuggled into her side. "You like it?"

"Oh, Temperance, it warms my soul. Mama would be so pleased."

"Mike has books, too." Tempy gazed at the shelf on the far wall with glee. Between them, they boasted nine books.

"Tempy, you brought good stuff from home." Eunice turned around. "Asa Pleasant whittles them swan-neck towel pegs, and that tatted dresser scarf couldn't have taken any room a-tall in your satchel. They make this place look dreadful fine."

"Lovejoy, will you weave me a flower

wreath? I'd like one over there." Tempy indicated a spot on the wall not far from a crate she'd covered with a green calico feed sack and used as a table to hold a kerosene lantern.

"Surely I will." Lovejoy didn't mention she'd just made one over at Daniel Chance's; she was just glad this one would be a welcome addition.

She went back to the main house to help fix supper and only half listened to the list of things the girls rattled off. They'd bought ammunition so the men could hunt, kerosene, wicks, molasses, paraffin. . . .

"So what do you think, Lovejoy?"

"Huh?" Lovejoy gave Lois a guilty look. "I confess, I got lost in my thoughts."

"I said, they built a smokehouse. Hezzy's takin' me huntin' tomorrow for black-tailed jackrabbits."

"Rabbit stew sounds mighty fine. I hope you come back with a whole slew of 'em."

"You're plum tuckered out, and we're talkin' your leg off." Tempy frowned. "You hungry?"

"Not in the least. I'm tired, though. Think I'll nap a bit." Accustomed to grabbing sleep when and where she could, Lovejoy curled up on a pallet in the corner and slipped off to sleep. The next thing she knew, a rooster crowed.

Tempy stirred and sat up. She turned and tucked the blanket back around Lovejoy's shoulders. "You sleep in. I'll see to breakfast."

Lovejoy thought to protest, then decided against it. She lay there and watched as her baby sister set to doing a woman's work. Her moves were sure and steady. Pride and pain warred in Lovejoy's heart.

Time's come. Time's come for me to let her fly. My baby sister's a full-growed woman, aglow with love. God, I'm askin' Thee to shine on her and the other gals. Let the happiness they have now last a lifetime. I'm thankin' Thee for answerin' my supplications for them — that they'd come and find men who'd be good husbands. Thou art faithful, Lord. Now holp me as I turn loose of them. Amen.

Eunice and Lois got up, primped a moment, then went to work. All three of them moved quietly in deference to the belief that Lovejoy was still asleep. While Lois went to gather eggs, Tempy and Eunice planned two supper menus — one if Lois and Hezzy brought back rabbit, another if they didn't.

"I brung my button tin. Obie's shirt was a-missin' a button last night. You gonna mind if'n he don't have on his shirt at breakfast so's I cain fix it? His other shirt's filthy."

"He can wear his Sunday best at the table," Tempy said in a muted tone. "We need to make our men new shirts."

Lovejoy squeezed her eyes shut tight to keep tears from overflowing. Tempy needed a new dress — really needed one; yet here she was, putting Mike's needs ahead of her own. Lovejoy had just enough of her own money to pay for her trip back home. *Pa gave me money when we left. . . .*

Lovejoy didn't know precisely how much money he'd given her. He'd shoved it into her hand, and she'd been afraid of any of the passengers on the train seeing her hold those greenbacks. Pretending to check on something in her medicine satchel, she'd stuffed the money into a small inside pocket. Since then she'd been so busy keeping an eye on the gals and on the folks over at Chance Ranch, Lovejoy hadn't troubled herself with seeing what she had.

Maybe if I'd have had me a new weddin' dress and spoken vows before a parson 'stead of having the judge pound his gavel and shoutin', "You're hitched," Vern might had honored our marriage.

Lovejoy sat up.

"You go on an' get a little more shut-eye."

Tempy wagged a spoon at her.

"Eunice, will you please get me my medicine satchel?"

Tempy's eyes widened. "Are you ailing? Did they have something catchy?"

"No, no. I'm fine." Lovejoy took her satchel from Eunice and gently worked the clasp until it opened. She pulled the paper money out of the pocket, yet kept the bills inside the bag. No use raising hopes prematurely. Could be they were nothing more than bank notes from somewhere back home — and those would be useless out here.

Peeping down into the dim satchel, Lovejoy smoothed a bill and felt her heart plummet. The Confederate note wasn't worth the paper it was printed on. *Good thing I didn't say anything to Tempy and get her hopes up for naught.*

Her fingers curled into a fist, crumpling the bill. Lovejoy started to withdraw her hand, but her heart skipped a beat when she spied a different bill. Legal Tender Note. This one was a Legal Tender Note. One whole dollar . . . and another . . . and a two-dollar note, too! Four dollars. She should hold one back to pay for food on the way home, but three dollars ought to buy enough material and ribbons to outfit all three brides.

Lois came in, set down the egg basket, and started to laugh. "We'd best make it a good breakfast. The menfolk are unhappy."

"Then why are you laughing?" Eunice gave her sister a baffled look.

" 'Cuz from the sounds of the bellowin' in the barn, they was all a-tryin' to wash up. Someone didn't latch a stall right, and a horse come over and drank up the water in the basin!"

They all started laughing, and Lois plopped into a chair. "I don't know if it was Obie or Hezzy —" She gulped in a breath and finished. "But he threatened to shave the horse's tail!"

"It had to be Mike. Obie and Hezzy have beards," Lovejoy pointed out.

Tempy whooped with laughter.

Hair combed and shirts tucked in, the men arrived for breakfast. Obie's upper lip bore stubble, and Mike's whole face looked like sandpaper.

Before everyone started eating, Lovejoy cleared her throat. "If'n y'all don't mind, I'd like to ask the blessin' this mornin'. Afore I do, I wanna say, I came here to be shore things'd work out — that these gals would be happy and you MacPhersons would treat 'em right. Well, I've come to a decision."

Lovejoy heard her sister suck in a quick breath.

Mike slipped his arm around Tempy's shoulders.

"For whatever it's worth, y'all have my blessing. But it's gotta be a real weddin' with all the trimmings. Onc't I got you all to the altar right, tight, and proper, I'll be headin' back home."

CHAPTER 12

"Hey there, Dan'l Chance. You're a hard-workin' man to be out so early of a mornin'."

Dan turned around and dipped his head in a curt greeting. "Mrs. Spencer."

"You come to gather mustard? Are the lassies ailin' again?"

"No." He felt utterly ridiculous standing there with an armful of bright yellow flowers. Because he didn't know diddly-squat about plants, he'd come to this spot because it was the only place he could be certain he'd harvest the right stuff. "Miriam wanted a supply to dry — just in case."

"She's a smart gal. I reckon you come to do the chore so's she cain keep an eye on all the Chance women." She didn't head straight for him. Instead, she veered to one side and clipped some leaves, zagged another way and plucked a few little flowers, then approached him.

He wasn't feeling overly talkative, but he managed another curt nod.

Lovejoy chatted as she wandered closer. " 'Tis a fine thing to hear your daughters are on the mend. I'm on my way to see how Delilah and Alisa are farin'."

"You're walking?"

"That's why God gave me feet."

"God made horses with four feet so they could go farther faster." As soon as he made that ridiculous comment, Dan fought the urge to make a strategic retreat. He'd already made an utter fool of himself.

She drew closer, and merriment sparkled in her eyes. "Tell you what, Dan'l Chance. If'n you don't tell that to the woolly worms, spiders, and centipedes, I won't. They all got plenty more feet than the both of us combined, but we got 'em beat in a race."

He let out a disbelieving laugh.

"Now don't you be a-laughin' at me, Dan'l." She continued to smile broadly and opened her gunnysack. "Woolly worms and me are right good friends. Their stripes always holp me decide what to gather on account they tell me how bad the winter's gonna be."

He accepted her implied invitation and dumped the mustard flowers into her sack. "You're friendly with worms?"

"You're friendly with horses," she countered with a feisty grin.

"I've seen you ride a horse." He tugged the bag from her and held it as she gathered more mustard. Her moves were spare and efficient. "You ought not be walking out here. It's not safe."

"I got my knife."

He resisted the urge to finger the hole in his hat that Delilah had put there with her knife. Of all the women he'd ever met, Daniel felt certain Lovejoy was probably the only other woman who could wield a knife with such speed and accuracy. Even so, that didn't count for much — not out here. "Snakes and bears wouldn't much care about your knife — not to mention the two-legged variety of wolves around here."

"You back to countin' legs again, cowboy?" She slanted him a quick look.

"Polly's learning her numbers."

"And her critters, too, from the way you're going about it."

"You're full of sass and vinegar, but this is a wild land. It takes more than a sharp tongue and a sharp knife to be safe." Taking her arm, he led her beside his horse. After shoving the nearly full bag back into her hands, he cinched his hands about her waist.

Lovejoy clamped her hands about his

wrists. "Wait just a minute, there. What're you up to?"

"One of us has to exercise some common sense."

"If'n you're so all-fired sure snakes are about, then why don't we share your horse? I cain ride pillion. You ride a grand horse. He shouldn't have no trouble with the extry weight."

"Fine." Dan turned loose of her, wondering what extra weight she meant. Lovejoy was a mere wisp of a woman. He didn't have all day to stand in a field of flowers jawing with a woman — however feisty or clever she might be. Leather stretched and eased as he swung himself into the saddle.

Spry as could be, Lovejoy simultaneously lifted her foot onto his and slipped her hand about his wrist. One small heft, and she swung up behind him. Her full skirts swirled with the action, then settled. She continued to clutch her bag in one arm and wound the other about his waist.

"You got this horse trained." Admiration filled her voice. "He didn't move an inch."

"I prize him." It was no understatement. Of all the brothers, Bryce had a knack with the beasts — but this horse was Daniel's. They'd taken a shine to each other from the start. "Cooper's good with my girls. Ginny

Mae has a habit of squealing, but he doesn't mind."

Lovejoy hadn't stretched the truth when she claimed she could ride pillion. Perched behind him, she not only kept balance but quickly sensed the horse's rhythm and moved naturally instead of going all stiff. It felt unsettling to have her arm about him, though. Other than his daughters' hugs, no one touched him.

"Why'd you name this here gelding Cooper?"

"After a Cooper's hawk."

"That 'cuz he moves so fast you pert near fly, or on account of his coat being the exact same shade of gray?"

"His coat."

"Don't the sun feel glorious?"

From the way her cheek brushed against his shirt, he could tell she'd turned her face upward. How many times a day did he do the same thing? Different as they were, it struck him that they were alike in such personal ways. They prized time alone in the morning and sun on their faces, and each had five siblings to love and worry about. She liked birds, too.

"Well, speakin' of hawks, looky there. That red-tailed hawk's ridin' a current. Powerful sight, ain't it? And hear that? You got

146

yourself a woodpecker!"

Dan didn't have much to say. The trip home was short, but in that time, Lovejoy identified several birdcalls and imitated them. "That 'un's a sparrow. Cain't tell from the sound if'n it's a Lincoln's sparrow, a house, or a fox sparrow. Surely ain't a song sparrow."

He didn't know, either. Dan pulled his horse to a quick halt as a covey of quail skittered by. "California quail. The meat's tender but gamey."

"It'd take a mess of them to feed a strappin' man like you. Do you set a box trap or do you net 'em?"

"Too much trouble to pluck them. We don't bother."

She managed to imitate several more birdcalls and viewed the landscape with unfeigned appreciation. *Not many women are content with such simplicity. It's a fine quality. Then again, from some of the comments she makes about life back home, Salt Lick Holler doesn't offer much.*

If any other woman told him she didn't want to remarry, he'd bet his bottom dollar she was lying. Violet Greene had come to town the same time Alisa did, and though her brother told all the men in Reliable that she was observing a year of mourning, the

147

only thing Dan thought she was observing were the men so she could weigh their worth. On the other hand, Lovejoy didn't seem to have a bit of guile in her. *She's a pleasure to have around.*

A few minutes later, just before they reached the barnyard, Lovejoy tugged on his shirt. "How 'bout you halt this horse out of sight? I aim to put my hand to work here. What say whilst I grab what b'longs to your lassies, you venture into your kid brothers' cabin and fetch me their dirty clothes? Ain't fittin' for me to prowl around there, and I aim to have the wash pot boilin' afore I give my greetings to the women. Thataway they cain't shilly-shally when I add in their laundry."

As plans went, it was a sound one. Selfless, too. Daniel remembered having to do the laundry before Miriam came to stay with them. It was a hot, tiresome, and thankless chore. "Okay. But I'll set the fire and fill the pot."

"Now there's the spirit!"

Lovejoy Spencer didn't believe in letting grass grow under her feet. By the time Dan had a fire set and the pot over the fresh flames, she'd exited the girls' cabin with her arms full. She hadn't just gathered clothes. She had towels and sheets, too. "How 'bout soap?" she whispered.

"Bryce keeps a supply in the tack room."

"Dandy. I'll fetch it."

He went into Bryce and Logan's cabin. By the time he'd plowed through the mess in his kid brothers' cabin and emerged, Lovejoy had finished shaving lye soap into the kettle. He gave the rope at her feet a glance. "It's an old myth that snakes won't cross a rope."

" 'Course that's a bunch of nonsense. I got me that length of rope thinkin' as fair a day as we got, I'll air out the blankets and quilts. I cain start at that far end of the clothesline, loop through the fork in yon tree, then —"

"I'll do it." As tasks went, it would take no time at all for him to rig the line; Lovejoy would have to climb the tree to wind a rope about the branches. She'd do it, too. Dan snatched the rope from the ground.

"I'd take it kindly if you'd string up the full length." She smiled as she dropped shirts into the wash water. "Get me near a kettle and a washboard, and I'm a wild woman."

"No one likes to do laundry."

"No one but me, then. It's a time to pray for the folks who wear the duds and thank God for His provision." She looked over at the cabins and nodded. "I reckon the kinfolk of yourn could use some prayers."

"They do plenty of praying."

Lovejoy gave him a long, shrewd look. "They do? You're not on speakin' terms with the Almighty?"

"No use talking to someone you don't trust."

"You surprise me, Dan'l. I figured you to be a man of his word and a believer."

He glowered at her. "I am."

"Now that don't make no sense a-tall. What're you doin', not talking to the Lord who holds your heart and soul?"

"He holds my wife." The raw words tore out of him.

Lovejoy stirred the wash with a wooden paddle that was as long as she was tall. "Not a one of us loses a loved one that we don't think God shoulda let us keep. Faith ain't a fair-weather thing. Fact is, faith is all we really, truly got."

"It wasn't all I had. I had a happy life with a woman I loved."

She bobbed her head in understanding. "Sad fact is, family, friends, possessions — they cain all be gone in an instant. That feller Job in the Bible found that out. If'n you meant it when you knelt at an altar and put your soul in God's hands, then you gotta leave it there. 'Specially when life brings hurts."

Daniel glowered at her. She thought having Hannah ripped from his life was simply a hurt?

"Grief's ugly. It bubbles up like this here lye soap. You cain swim in grief for a time and come out clean, or you cain stew until it eats at your seams and tears you to shreds." She lifted a shirt, inspected it, and dunked it back in. "Mayhap I was wrong. I come here today to wash and pray for the womenfolk. P'rhaps 'tis you I'm supposed to be holding up to Jesus."

"If all it took to make your grief go away were a couple of prayers, then you must not have loved your husband the way I loved my wife."

Lovejoy didn't say a word. She set down the paddle and walked off.

Daniel paced over and knotted the rope to the end of the clothesline stake. *Mousy hillbilly woman doesn't know what she's talking about. Simple things like plants and laundry are fine for her, but that's her limit. So what if she can ride both pillion and alone?* He paced several feet, passed the rope through the fork of a tree, and wound it twice so it'd stay taut. A voice deep inside taunted, *Hannah never learned to drive a*

wagon, let alone ride. He banished that
frustrating memory and reminded himself
that Hannah was a lady. *So what if Lovejoy
can copy the whistle of every bird in the township?* He headed toward another tree. *No
lady whistles.*

*Anyone can go pick mustard and make a
poultice.* The rope burned through his hands
as he savagely yanked it around a branch.
*Hannah never did — not even when Polly was
Caleb's age and sick like this. Well, Miriam
hasn't ever made her baby son a plaster . . .
actually, she did fix a turpentine one.*

No matter what thought registered, a
contradiction followed. None of those
counterpoints portrayed Hannah as a paragon. All along he'd been remembering her
as the perfect wife and mother. But in the
last week, he'd had memories of a woman
who had both strengths and flaws. Instead
of being a paragon, she'd been . . . well,
she'd been the woman he'd married and
loved.

Lovejoy's soft, hillbilly twang haunted
him. *You cain stew until it eats at your seams
and tears you to shreds.* Wasn't that the very
nature of grief? It was impossible to lose a
love and still be whole.

Lovejoy's words echoed in his mind. *A*

man of his word and a believer . . . not talking to the Lord who holds your heart and soul?

He finished stringing the extensive clothesline and called himself ten kinds of fool for bringing her here. He picked up his ax and headed for trees that needed to be cleared. That odd little woman could fuss over everyone else — she'd just better keep away from him.

CHAPTER 13

"There." Lovejoy smoothed the quilt in place on Miriam and Gideon's bed and straightened up. "Now where was I?"

"You were telling about Tempy's wedding dress," Delilah prompted as she tugged at the other side of the quilt. They'd gone from cabin to cabin, putting the fresh linens and aired blankets back on the beds. Miriam had helped with all the other beds, but Caleb decided he was hungry, so she sat in the rocker to nurse him while Delilah stepped up to help.

"Tempy and Eunice and Lois is all getting married," Polly said importantly. "I know 'bout weddings 'cuz Auntie Miri-Em had a wedding and so did Auntie 'Lilah. Auntie 'Lisa got married in San Fur-isco."

Lovejoy smiled. "Oh, that's right. Well, that dress — it's dreadfully beautiful. Brings tears to my eyes just thinkin' on it."

Alisa finished pulling a sun-baked case on

a pillow. "She'll make a lovely bride."

"They all will. Smart, too. Did I tell you 'bout what they done for the fabric? I cain't recollect who I tole what to."

Alisa folded a towel and slipped it on the towel rod at the side of the washstand. "You made me take a nap. I haven't heard a word about the weddings."

"You needed that nap." Delilah frowned at Alisa. "Titus said just the other day that you're not sleeping well."

Lovejoy folded her arms akimbo. "Alisa, I aim to tell your man he needs to hog-tie you. Them ankles of yourn are too swoll up."

"You said it was all right for them to be puffy."

"That was when they was turnip sized. You're up to muskmelon, and I aim to put a stop to it. If'n that was all, I'd be holdin' my peace, but them hands o' yourn are plumpin' up."

Alisa looked down and fiddled with her wedding band. "Miriam said her ring got tight when she was carrying Caleb."

Miriam looked at Alisa's hands and gasped. "Not tight like that!"

Lovejoy pursed her lips and waited a few moments. "You wantin' me to spout off platitudes so's you'll stop worryin', or you want me to speak the truth?"

"You not a spout. You a girl." Ginny Mae gave her a perplexed look.

"I am?" Lovejoy made a show of spreading her skirts and looking down. "Well, fancy that. I am! Since we've settled that, why don't you take me to the kitchen so's we cain finish makin' supper?"

" 'Kay." Ginny Mae took her hand and led her through the doorway.

Lovejoy shot a look over her shoulder at Alisa and mouthed, "Later."

Not long thereafter, Lovejoy put some lemonade in front of Delilah and a cup of tea down for Alisa. "You gals drink up."

Delilah sipped from her glass. "The lemon's such a big help. As long as Paul keeps me in lemon drops, I'm not nearly as queasy."

As if on cue, Paul came in. "You talking about me, darlin'?" He gave her a kiss on the cheek.

"Unca Paul, Miss Lovejoy's going to spout on Auntie 'Lisa." Polly wound her arms around his thighs. "Did you come to watch?"

Paul's brows furrowed.

"I'll be speaking to Mrs. Chance alone," Lovejoy announced.

"They's all Mrs. Chances, Miss Lovejoy. Which one you wanna talk to alone?"

"Why does Lovejoy need to speak with someone alone? What's wrong?" Gideon clomped into the room with Titus on his heels. He sucked in a loud breath. "The last time she took one of you aside, it was to tell Delilah —" He turned to his wife. "Miriam, are we going to have another one already?"

"Miriam's in the family way again?" Logan let out a low whistle.

"No! No, I'm not." Miriam glowed with embarrassment.

"Then what is it?" Titus stepped over toward Alisa and gave her a stern look. "You're too pale."

"You all sit down and eat. We got a nice meal a-waitin' for —"

"Lovejoy Spencer," Titus growled, "don't you dare think you'll get us to ignore something by waving food under our noses. It won't work."

Miriam let out a mirthless laugh. "Unless it's cobbler or gingerbread."

"Or —"

"Alisa." Titus's voice halted her from adding to the list. "Now what's going on?"

"Good thing 'bout big families is they care; bad thing 'bout big families is they hover." Lovejoy bustled through them and thumped the coffeepot down on the table. "Nobody's entitled to know nothin' that somebody wants to keep secret about their body."

"Huh?" Bryce gave Logan a bewildered look. "Did that make sense to you?"

"Someone's keeping secrets about bodies," Logan answered.

"What's this about secrets and bodies?" Dan straggled in and swept Ginny Mae into his arms and held her protectively. "Was someone done in?"

"Bloodthirsty lot, these Chance men," Lovejoy muttered as she headed toward the stove. When she turned back with a bowl of zucchini in her hands, an arc of men surrounded her.

"We decided something today," Gideon started.

"You're staying here." Titus added, "After your sister's wedding."

"Our wives need you. The children need you." Paul took the bowl from her and handed it to Logan, who promptly passed it to Bryce. "You can't go."

"We voted." Bryce swiped a slice of the vegetable and popped it into his mouth before setting the bowl aside.

"And you thought I didn't make sense?" Lovejoy gawked at them. "You cain't go voting on makin' a body stay someplace."

"Sure we can." Titus shrugged. "We've

done it three times already. You're the fourth."

"Y'all voted?" Lovejoy couldn't fathom this turn of events.

"All but Dan. He was off choppin' wood. Don't matter, anyway. All five of us agreed, and the ladies already made their wishes clear. Majority rules."

"Dan would vote for you to stay." Paul's voice carried grave, unwavering certainty. "He knows what it's like for a man to worry about his wife during her carrying months. He'd want you here for Alisa and Delilah's birthings."

"You said you have someone back home filling in as the healer," Miriam interrupted.

"The very woman who trained you," Delilah added. "So you have every confidence in her ability. She'll take care of them; you'll be here to take care of us."

"Ain't right for me to presume on Widow Hendricks."

Daniel hadn't joined his brothers when they surrounded her. That fact hadn't escaped Lovejoy's notice. He'd stayed back by the door holding Ginny Mae. The man still looked as bleak as he had when he stomped away this morning; nonetheless, he locked gazes with Lovejoy. "You're needed here. I'll send a telegram."

"Where did all these come from?" Daniel stared at the wagon Lovejoy drove into the yard. Hannah always bemoaned the dearth of flowers in California, but Lovejoy managed to fill the entire buckboard with blossoms.

"They're all about you." Lovejoy swept her hand toward the pastures. "Poppies everywhere, curly dock, fern, and daisies. Pretty as it is, mustard don't seem quite right for a weddin', so I didn't go for any of it. Found me a passel of pasture roses, seep monkeyflower, elderberry. Delilah offered anything we wanted to cut from her flower garden, too."

He checked to be sure Lovejoy set the brake, afraid she'd been so excited about the blossoms that she'd forgotten something basic — only she'd been diligent. "Where do you want the flowers?"

She laughed. "Alisa's cabin, if you please. She and Delilah are gonna holp arrange them. The both of them have an eye for beauty."

"What's this?" He thumped on a closed crate.

"Vittles. The gals are bringin' up more in

t'other wagon. Did I remember to thankee for having the grooms come set up the benches? Couldn't abide having them shuffle 'round there today. Men shouldn't see their bride on the weddin' day afore they reach the altar."

Like a hen with too many chicks, Lovejoy squawked and scurried about all morning long. Daniel minded his daughters because Miriam and Lovejoy were busy icing the wedding cake. By noontime, neighbors filled the benches, and the parson stood up front.

Lovejoy sat off to the side up front, her dulcimer in her lap and a wreath of flowers on her head. Her light brown hair shone in the sun. In the weeks that she'd been here, she'd had enough to eat, and it showed in the soft curve of her cheeks, the sheen of her hair, and the feminine form filling her dress.

Her dress. She'd changed to her other dress — the one Daniel knew was her Sunday best. The woman owned two gowns, both worn beyond redemption. He'd already spied the brides. They all wore new gowns — Lois in yellow, Eunice in green, and Tempy in blue. Why didn't Lovejoy get a new dress for herself? She needed one.

Someone must have gotten hold of Parson Abe's black suit, because it was neatly pressed instead of rumpled. He stood up front and nodded at Lovejoy. Once she started strumming her dulcimer and singing, the MacPherson men lined up at the altar. All three wore love-struck smiles.

Weddings. The " 'til death us do part" promise of his wedding vows came far too soon, and seeing others find love and expect a long, happy future made his heart ache. How could God give love, only to take it away?

Daniel hadn't attended Gideon and Miriam's wedding, because it was just too painful to remember the day when he and Hannah took their own vows. When Titus and Alisa got married in San Francisco, relief flooded Daniel. He'd been spared having to decide how to handle another ceremony and managed to put in an appearance at the reception they'd held back here at the ranch two weeks later. That should have been enough, but it wasn't. In a rash moment, he'd promised Paul that he'd escort Delilah down the aisle. He kept his word, but that stretched him to the limit.

Flowers and rings, vows and kisses — he knew firsthand those sacred moments truly forged two hearts into one. He also knew the pain of having death tear that heart asunder.

"We're ready now!" Ginny Mae's excited squeal loosened the tension.

Dan stood toward the back and couldn't help smiling when Polly and Ginny Mae started down the aisle. Each held a basketful of flower petals. Polly strewed hers with notable grace; Ginny Mae picked up clumps and dumped them onto the ground every now and then.

He squinted, then his smile nearly cracked his sun-weathered face. Instead of tying ribbons on the handle of Ginny Mae's basket as she had with Polly's, Lovejoy had wound wire or thread around a little brownish-black something-or-other to make one of Ginny Mae's beloved "worms."

Woolly worm aside, the color plan suddenly made sense — Polly in pink, Ginny in lavender, and the brides all lined up . . . a rainbow of pastels.

He looked at Lovejoy. One stripe short of the rainbow. It was how she had described the land, but at the moment, it also explained the wedding party. Well, that rainbow was missing a color. Something . . . orangish. Maybe the color of a peach or apricot or, well, anyway, a dress out of that would have suited Lovejoy.

Only she didn't seem to mind the fact that her gown looked as exciting as mud. As the brides and grooms paired up, she softly plucked the strings of her dulcimer and started to sing a hymn.

"By vows of love together bound,
   The twain, on earth, are one;
One may their hearts, O Lord, be found,
   Till earthly cares are done."

Since Obie was the eldest, the parson had him and his bride speak their vows first. Once the ring was on Lois's hand, Lovejoy sang the next verse of the hymn.

"As from the home of earlier years
   They wander hand in hand,
To pass along, with smiles and tears,
   The path of Thy command."

Hezzy and Eunice came next. Hezzy wouldn't let go of her hand long enough to slip the ring in place, so the parson helpfully accomplished that task.

"With more than earthly parents' care,
   Do Thou their steps attend;
And with the joys or woes they share,
   Thy loving kindness blend."

Mike and Tempy came last. Ginny Mae tugged on the parson's pant leg. "Him not

Micah. Him Mike." Likewise, "Her Tempy, not 'Rance." The congregation muffled chuckles. Daniel didn't bother. He laughed aloud.

Instead of being weepy, Lovejoy beamed at her baby sister's wedding, and as soon as Daniel started laughing, Lovejoy looked into his eyes and laughed, too. She quickly regained her composure and sang the next verse as the parson served Holy Communion to the couples.

"O let the memory of this hour
　　In future years come nigh
To bind, with sweet, attractive power,
　　And cheer them till they die."

The hymn had been downright nice up till that last line. Then Daniel decided Lovejoy exercised lousy judgment in her choice of music.

"You MacPherson men may greet your brides."

"It's about time!" Obie shouted as he yanked Lois into his arms.

Everyone cheered as the newly wedded couples kissed.

"Wait a minute. My turn!" Polly motioned to Davy Greene.

Daniel took a second to realize his daughter thought she was going to either kiss or marry that snot-nosed, spoiled brat of a kid. He hiked up the aisle just as Davy reached Polly's side. Bending down so he rested his hands on his knees, he said very distinctly to the chunky kid, "Go back and sit with your mama."

Polly's face lit up. "You wanna marry me, Daddy?"

"I wanna marry Daddy." Ginny Mae glowered at Polly.

"I married your mama. She was the only bride I'll ever have." He scooped them up in his arms.

"Parson," Lovejoy called out, "how 'bout if you declare Dan'l Chance and those lassies father and daughters?"

Parson Abe cleared his throat, and his voice deepened to sound important. "I now pronounce you father and daughters. You girls each kiss your papa."

His daughters both placed a peck on his cheeks. Dan gave them each a squeeze and a kiss. He was glad he'd come to the wedding, after all.

CHAPTER 14

"He slept through the night," Miriam whispered as she tiptoed into the room.

Lovejoy chortled softly as she finished changing Caleb's diaper. "You talkin' 'bout your son or your man?"

"Both!" Miriam yawned. "I did, too. What did you do?"

"Not a thing. That's the trick. At his age, he don't need to suckle at night. He just got used to wakin' up and wantin' company. He fussed a moment, then decided since nobody was a-gonna pay him no mind, he'd lief as well go back to sleep." Lovejoy handed the baby to his mother. "He's hungry as cain be."

Miriam took her son to her bedroom, and soon the homey creak of a rocking chair filled the cabin. Lovejoy washed up, got dressed, then plaited her hair.

Somewhere along the line, someone had mentioned they'd recently doubled the size of this cabin — mostly because with the brothers marrying and neighbors dropping by, Paul had built a much-needed second dining table. Adding on allowed a small parlor and let Gideon and Miriam have a room that would be for their children. Lovejoy had moved into that nursery and shared it with Caleb.

She scanned the room and wrinkled her nose at her reflection over the washbowl. Though never one to put on airs or long for fancy things, she was the sorriest lookin' woman in the county. All the Chance women wore their hair pinned up, and once Tempy and the gals went to town, they'd followed suit. *My hair looks like a silty river a-runnin' down my spine bone.*

Since I don't care to catch myself a husband, my appearance don't much matter, but it surely would be wondrous to move and talk so ladylike. These here women are like queens. Lovejoy laughed at herself. None of that mattered. When she went home, those kinds of trappings and pretenses would be out of place. *Who am I kiddin'? I'm just an ol' hillbilly woman, and a plain one at that.* She tied on her boots and went to see about starting breakfast.

As she cooked, she asked Delilah, "Why do ya'll go a-buyin' what grows free?"

"Like what?" Delilah started setting the tables.

"Yarbs and such. Thyme, sage, rosemary — why, you could have nice, fresh stuff 'stead of this bitty box you got at the mercantile."

Delilah laughed. "The MacPhersons gave me a bag of seeds for my birthday. Paul and I planted most of the flowers, but I didn't know what to do with the herbs."

"Yore lookin' pert today. What say we fix up a yarb garden?"

"Oh, I'd love that. I enjoy gardening so much!"

By afternoon Delilah, Lovejoy, Polly, and Ginny Mae were dirt-streaked and delighted. They shared a pitcher of lemonade and watched Shortstack stalk Daniel as he put up a chicken-wire fence around the carefully laid-out plot. "How's about we go for a nice walk? I been readin' that book Paul got me from town. I'm thinkin' we cain gather up some of the edibles and usables."

Daniel straightened up. "Usables?"

"That book Paul got me in town says there's plenty hereabouts that's handy if a body knows what to do with it. Yesterday I seen a bunch of broom. Broom's wild, and I reckon we cain gather up sufficient for me to make up some brooms — maybe even little ones for small hands." She cast a smile at his daughters.

"Poison oak's bad this year," he warned. "No going off the path."

"I'll take good care of yore loved ones, Dan'l."

"But who's going to take care of you?"

Lovejoy slid her hands down her skirt. "You needn't fret o'er that. The dear Lord does a fine job."

Daniel watched them go. Delilah and Polly held hands, and each swung a basket in the other hand. Lovejoy carried Ginny Mae on her left hip and carried both a bucket and her ever-present gunnysack. Suspecting Lovejoy would find things she wanted to transplant, he shifted the fence line she'd paced off. Five more feet wouldn't make a hill of beans' worth difference to him, but she'd be pleased.

And he wanted to do things for her.

Lovejoy had faith God would take care of her soul, but that woman needed someone to fill in the little things here on earth. Self-reliant as she might be, that mountain girl needed to learn that others could help her so she didn't have to scrape by. She put her heart and hands to helping others, and the result was she didn't pay much attention to her own needs.

She'd come here and quietly filled in wherever they needed her. Before they'd moved here, Ma had an herb garden. It would be a nice sight, and he recalled how flavorful her cooking had been. She would have loved knowing the place boasted an herb — or as Lovejoy called it, a yarb — garden. Lovejoy was full of ideas and nifty tricks.

Her latest idea to make little brooms for his daughters was charming. As soon as he finished the fence, he'd go find saplings or thin branches that he could whittle into broomsticks. Maybe he'd whittle a special hook for her medicine satchel. She was always careful to put it up high, out of the girls' reach. The brass latch on that satchel had been hanging by a small wire she'd threaded through where the prongs had been, but he'd repaired it good as new last night with four small brads and a reinforcing plate. He wondered when she'd discover that. It wouldn't be a secret when she did. Lovejoy noticed little things and always appreciated them.

"Hey, Dan!"

Daniel turned toward the stable. He didn't see anyone, but it had been Bryce's voice.

"The blue's in a bad way." For Bryce to

call out a problem meant something was drastically wrong. He normally doctored the animals by himself.

Dan left the bright summer sun and entered the cool shade of the barn. They'd sunk a tidy sum into buying the blue roan last week. For being just weaned, it already stood twelve hands and boasted a sweet disposition. They had big plans for him. "What's wrong?"

"Colic." Bryce grunted.

Daniel immediately grabbed the halter and started pulling. "I'll walk him."

Bryce eased away. "Have at it. He's been fighting me."

Clenching the halter tighter, Daniel hauled the beast up the center aisle of the barn to the doorway and back. They paced that same route several times. He kept his gait steady and slow, careful not to exhaust Blue.

"I already gave him hot water and mineral oil," Bryce said.

It took the two of them to keep Blue upright. The colt tried desperately to lie down so he could roll, but that would be the death of him. His coat grew slick and dark with sweat.

"He's sufferin' something awful," Bryce said as he tried to wipe down the horse.

Daniel heard the edge in Bryce's voice.

172

Calm as Bryce stayed in the worst of cases when the animals sickened, that boded ill. "Walking isn't working." Unable to think of anything else to do, Daniel asked, "Think we ought to give him another dose of mineral oil?"

"I gave him plenty. It didn't work. Only thing left is an old horseman's remedy."

"We're going to lose him if we don't do something quick. Let's do it."

Miriam came into the stable. "Did you need some lunch or help?"

"Coffee. Strong as you've got it," Bryce ordered. "I want two quarts. Ginger tea, too. Same two quarts."

Miriam got a puzzled look on her face, but she didn't stay to ask why he'd made such an odd request. Something in his tone sent her flying.

"Keep him upright," Bryce said. "I need whiskey."

"Bryce, drinking —"

"For the horse." Bryce shot him an irritated look and headed toward the tack room. When he came back with two sizable bottles, he added, "Seein' Logan fall off his horse and brain Miriam the night she arrived should have made me swear off the stuff. I was too hardheaded to figure it out, but being drunk as a skunk when Titus brought Alisa here finally made me see the light. I haven't had a drop since. I keep a store of it for medicinal purposes."

Miriam reappeared bearing the coffeepot. Alisa accompanied her with a pitcher. "Lovejoy made ginger tea for us this morning."

"Empty them on in here." Bryce had taken the caps off both bottles and was dumping their contents into a steel bucket.

Fearing the horse might kick one of the women, Daniel rasped, "You women best get out of here."

"We'll be praying," Alisa said as she and Miriam scurried away.

Pouring the remedy into a suffering colt took brute strength and perseverance. As soon as they succeeded, Daniel and Bryce started the horse in motion again.

"How long before we know if that worked?" Daniel looked over the colt's withers at Bryce for the answer.

"Twenty minutes or so." Bryce's brow furrowed. "It's amazing that we already had that ginger tea. Coffee, we always have, but the tea . . . well, that was nothing short of heavenly providence."

"Lovejoy made it."

Bryce rubbed the blue as they shuffled along. His voice was slow and thoughtful.

"Never seen a woman like her."

"She's one of a kind."

"You startin' to have feelin's for her, Dan?"

Dan snapped, "I've already had a good woman."

"Yup, you did." A second later Bryce added, "Good, not perfect. Hannah loved you, and she bore you two children."

Chest tight, Daniel waited for the other shoe to drop.

"I won't recite her shortcomings, Dan. I'm just going to say she had some. We all do. Grieving makes us remember folks fondly."

"There's nothing wrong with that."

Bryce heaved a sigh. "Tell me, which horse is better? This here blue or Cooper?"

"What kind of nonsense is that? This one is young and untried. He's worth a bundle. Cooper is trained and useful. He's proven himself over and over. They're entirely different. I can't compare them."

"Hannah was like this blue — beautiful, sleek, and young. She meant the world to you. Lovejoy's like Cooper — ordinary, hardworking, and loyal, but you're blind to that. She can't measure up because you've let your memories turn a regular woman into a saint."

"Who says I'm blind?" As soon as the words were out of his mouth, Dan stopped in his tracks. He stared at his brother. "I can list plenty of Lovejoy's virtues. It doesn't mean I'm ready to get hitched to her, though."

"I didn't ask if you were ready to get hitched. I asked if you're startin' to have feelings."

At that moment the blue managed to get down to business. Bryce nodded wearily. "He'll make it. I'll keep him walking awhile yet. You can go on."

Dan headed toward the wide-open door. He stopped in the big sunlit square and looked out. His daughters both wore wreaths of daisies in their hair and about their necks, and they each had hold of Lovejoy's skirts. Drawing in a deep breath, Dan turned back toward Bryce. "Yeah. I've got feelings for her."

CHAPTER 15

"Reliable is one fine little place," Tempy said as she latched a lid on a jar of berries.

"Purdy as a fawn's coat." Lovejoy scooted over and made room for Delilah at the table. Two days ago the Chance women had gone to the MacPherson spread to help put up vegetables. Today the MacPherson women were returning the favor after they'd all gone berry picking.

"And the folks hereabouts are neighborly as cain be." Lois came out of the bedroom carrying Caleb, with Ginny Mae and Polly following behind her. The children's cheeks were flushed from their nap.

Reba White had come, too. Priscilla refused to join them, but no one pointed that out. Lovejoy had learned Priscilla had refused Titus's marriage proposal, so she figured it was for the best that Alisa wouldn't have to spend an awkward day with a disagreeable woman.

The Chance families couldn't begin to imagine how blessed they were to have tables laden with plenty and not know what it was to be hungry, to sit at that table where love, not strife, ruled. Lovejoy smiled at Tempy. The true blessing was that her own sister had married up, and the Lord seemed to be smiling down on her in the same way.

A knock sounded on the open door as someone said, "Is Miz Spencer here?"

"Yes, she is, Todd." Miriam motioned her neighbor to come inside.

"I heard tell she's good at doctoring. Chris Roland got a gash on his head that needs stitching."

Wiping her hands on her apron, Lovejoy headed toward the bedroom. "Let me get my satchel."

"What do you mean, you let her ride off with him?" Daniel glowered at his brothers as they got ready to sit down to supper. "This can't continue. Two days can't pass without someone wanting her attention."

Gideon elbowed Titus. "It's mostly Dan's fault. Chopping all that wood, he gets some pretty wicked splinters."

Daniel ignored that jibe. "If folks want Lovejoy's help, they can come here instead of expecting her to wander all over Reliable

178

Township. It's not safe."

"She's scrappy." Bryce plopped down and swiped a biscuit. "I reckon she can handle herself."

Logan snorted. "He reckons anyone who can lance a boil on a horse can do anything."

Paul cast a quick glance at Delilah and whispered hotly, "Watch what you say. Delilah's barely keeping her meals down. I won't have you spoil her appetite."

"Well, I'm taking a stand," Daniel announced. "She doesn't pay house calls unless it's an emergency, and if that's what's up, one of us men will escort her."

He kept busy with his daughters at the table, then took them to their cabin. It didn't surprise him in the least when Lovejoy knocked on the door. "I come to smear some salve on the girls' arms. They got scratched up a mite pickin' berries today."

Daniel stood back and watched Lovejoy minister to his daughters. Once he'd thought her to be a mousy-looking woman. He couldn't have been more wrong. Compassion shone from her hazel eyes, and her mouth perpetually tilted into a warm smile. The string she used to tame her hair into a simple plait snagged on a button of Polly's nightdress and slipped off. Instead of fussing with her own hair, Lovejoy fretted over a scratch on Polly's arm then kissed it better. Dan caught himself wishing the braid would unravel entirely.

"There, now. Sweet dreams, lassies." Lovejoy turned and pulled one of her dynamite vials out of her satchel. "You'll probably need this."

"What is it?"

"Dr. J. H. McLeans Volcanic Oil Liniment. I poured half into this for you and gave the bottle to Bryce. After fighting that colicky colt yesterday, it stands to reason yore shoulders might be squawkin' a mite."

"I take care of myself. I don't need you to coddle me."

Polly sat up in the bed. "Miss Lovejoy cuddles good, Daddy. Why don't you want her to cuddle you?"

He said coddle, not cuddle. It means to fuss and pamper, Pollywog. I don't expect no one's gonna cuddle your pa, on account of him bein' prickly as a berry bramble.

Lovejoy woke early the next morning and groaned over the memory of what she'd said to Polly last night. If she hadn't given her word that she'd stay and help Delilah and Alisa with their birthings, she'd gladly pack her bags and run off.

Facing Daniel after she'd said that was

180

going to test her composure. *Why is he different from every other man? I cain hold my own with any other buck in the world, but Dan — well, he just manages to take me by surprise.*

She dressed and searched in vain for another scrap of string to tie her plait.

Miriam slipped into the room. "I thought I heard Caleb."

"He'd jist started stirrin' a bit." Lovejoy lifted him from his cradle. "He's a fine boy."

Miriam took him and rubbed noses with her son. "That's because you take after your daddy, don't you?"

The one thing Lovejoy missed about Salt Lick Holler was that she never had any solitude. Why, back home, when she was feelin' a mite blue, she could go out all on her lonesome and natter with God about her achy heart. Most days she felt happy with her lot in life, but every now and again she struggled with being a lonesome, barren woman surrounded by blossoming families. Watching the folks at the MacPherson and Chance ranches hip-deep in love . . . well, now that was a right wondrous thing. But it also hurt. Times like this, her arms ached to hold a young'un of her own, and there were times she wished she wouldn't be going back home to an empty house.

But what about how I acted last night? I could end up just as bitter as Daniel if I let this briar patch of self-pity hold me fast.

"It looks to be a fine morn. I'm gonna go gathering."

"Why don't you wait till after breakfast? Delilah or I could go with you."

Lovejoy shook her head. "No need." She slipped her knife in her sheath and hastened away before Miriam asked any questions.

"Lovejoy didn't go pay a house call on anyone, did she? It's not like her to leave others to do the cooking."

"Are you kidding?" Gideon gave Daniel a cocky grin. "We know better than to let her off the property without your approval."

"She went to gather more 'yarbs,' " Miriam said. "Don't worry. She has her knife, and one of the dogs was trotting alongside her."

Miriam looked at Delilah and Alisa. "Do either of you have any fabric? Lovejoy's dresses are in tatters."

"I'm doing nothing but sitting around." Alisa perked up. "I can sew for her."

"I'm goin' to town." Bryce propped his elbows on the table. "I suppose I could get material."

Dan nearly choked on his coffee.

Logan hooted as the women exchanged horrified looks.

"Mrs. White would help me," Bryce muttered.

"Fine. Have her help you." Dan nodded curtly. "Get something pretty — orange and flowery." He stood abruptly, suddenly feeling ridiculous. As if to provide an excuse, he tacked on, "She won't take payment for healing my girls. At least this way I can cover my debt."

Paul elbowed Delilah. "We owe her, too. Are you going to be picky about the color?"

"I'll go along and see what she has."

The table conversation ebbed and flowed. Daniel ignored it and secretly hoped Lovejoy hadn't gotten lost. The woman didn't seem to possess much of a sense of direction. By midmorning he couldn't stand it anymore. Lovejoy hadn't returned — he'd been keeping a lookout for her and determined it was time he tracked her down. What if a snake bit her or she fell and got hurt?

Daniel followed her tracks. It wasn't hard at all. Lovejoy wore sturdy, albeit badly worn, boots. The Chance women all had dainty lady's shoes that left narrow heel imprints; Lovejoy's small footprint was the only one with a broad heel. It wasn't long before he discovered where she'd gone.

Her gunnysack bulged with whatever she'd harvested, and a pail of berries sat beside it, but for the first time ever, he saw Lovejoy sitting still. The woman was always in motion — working, helping, rocking a baby. Even for church, she'd either play her dulcimer or keep one of his girls content on her lap. The oldest mutt they had lay with his head in her lap, but she wasn't stroking him. Something was wrong.

CHAPTER 16

"Lovejoy?"

Her posture straightened, but she didn't turn around.

Dan hastened closer and noticed the distinctive motion a woman used to secretly wipe away tears. "Did you get hurt?"

She shook her head and wouldn't meet his gaze.

Dan couldn't very well ignore her red eyes and tearstained face. He didn't know what to say, though. *Talk is overrated.* He'd forgotten his father's tenet until now, but it fit. Sometimes talk just didn't suit the situation and wouldn't improve it any.

Dan sat beside Lovejoy under the tree, reached over, and silently pulled her into the lee of his body. It was a bittersweet time, her resting against him, neither of them saying a word. Somehow they were sharing the deep hurts of life. After a while, Lovejoy took a deep breath, but he didn't let go.

185

"Some days are rougher than others, aren't they?"

She nodded.

"I got mouthy last night when you were trying to be kind. I said harsh words, and it made things harder for you. It's not you. It's me."

Well, isn't that just the way God works? She'd just about given up hope of being around Daniel — not in a romantic way but just as a friend — and here he'd sought her out, waded in the creek of sorrow along with her, and given consolation. Pa and her husband always blamed her, told her everything was her fault. Here Dan sat a-sayin' 'twas his doing.

"I get upset, and I chop wood." He cupped her head to his chest. "You can't go tromping off when you're uneasy. It just isn't safe. I'll put a bench by the tree at the curve in the creek. You can go sit there when you need a spell."

She eased away from him. " 'Tisn't necessary. I won't be stayin' all that long, Dan'l."

"I'll do it because I want to." He brushed her cheek with his thumb. "Now let's take you home."

When she stood, her hair unraveled more. Only a soiled dove went about with her hair all wild. Lovejoy grabbed it, quickly twisted it, and jammed a twig through to keep the heavy tresses at her nape.

Daniel pulled it out. "Don't go putting an ugly stick in such pretty hair."

Lovejoy couldn't think of a reply to make to such an outrageous comment. Daniel had just proven himself to be a man who could own up to his flaws and share someone's sorrows without prying. For him to pay her a compliment was like . . . well, sort of like sprinkling sugar atop a pie even though it wasn't needed. She smiled at that thought because Daniel's flattery was especially sweet. No one else had ever spoken a word of praise about her appearance. She'd cherish those words for the rest of her days.

Once they got back to the barnyard, Dan followed her into the house. "Miriam, how are we set for ribbons?"

"The girls have plenty. Why?"

"Lovejoy needs some for her plait." He turned to leave then said over his shoulder, "And don't go trying to put it up all fancy."

As the day progressed, Lovejoy heard him sawing and hammering. Late in the afternoon he popped Ginny Mae onto his shoulders. "Polly, take Lovejoy's hand and come see what Daddy did."

They walked to the bend in the creek, and

Lovejoy let out a cry of surprise. Dan grinned at her. When he said he'd put a bench there, she simply assumed he'd drag one of the benches they kept in the barn and used for church meetings. Only the church benches didn't have a back to them.

"You built those!" He'd not built one small bench or chair by the tree; he'd made three benches.

"Yep. You're going to stay until the babies are born, so it's only right that there are seats for when your sister and friends come to visit."

"Oh, Dan. Thankee."

"Nothin' better than fresh air and sunshine to perk up a body." Lovejoy sat back on her heels and lifted her face to the sky. "Ever think on how God made light first?"

"Can't say that I have." Delilah dusted off her hands. "Until this year, I didn't even believe in Him. It's a wonder they took me in. I couldn't cook, garden, or pray."

"Seems to me you've learnt plenty." Lovejoy reached over and patted Delilah's tummy. "And you're gonna be a good mama and teach your young'un all those things."

"You'll have to teach me that trick you used so Miriam's baby sleeps through the night."

"Time did that, I didn't. A babe's born wee little, so his belly cain't hold much. Give him three, mebbe four moons, and he fills up right fine and cain make it through. Caleb's next fit'll come when he's a-fixin' to cut teeth. I'll check in that book your man give me. See if'n there's sommat growin' hereabouts to holp with that."

"We have plenty of time," Miriam said.

"Not by my reckonin'. I aim to spend the next week or so gathering." Lovejoy plucked a sprig of mint, dusted it off on her sleeve, popped it between her teeth, and bit. The taste burst in her mouth. "Moon's on the rise, so the flow tide in the stems will make the flowers and leaves best to pluck."

"Daniel's likely to throw another fit if you go out at night." Delilah giggled. "He about pounded a hole in our door when he couldn't find you."

"I have to agree with him," Miriam defended. "It didn't seem wise to go out on a moonless night."

"Dark is when the roots are strongest." Lovejoy shrugged. "It's jist a fact — like putting in the root vegetables for cold seasons and above-the-ground crops during summer. There's still plenty of room in the loft for me to dry things. I'm trying to put by plenty for Tempy and for you folks as well as gather up stores for folks back home."

"Won't the lady who's filling in for you do that for the people in Salt Lick?" Alisa sat in the shade. The curls around Ginny Mae's face danced in the breeze Alisa's fan stirred up.

"Widow Hendricks is nigh unto fifty. She's got rickety bones and her back's twistin' like a gnarled tree."

"If you show us what you need, we can help gather," Delilah offered.

"Might be I'd take Miriam up on that offer, but you and Alisa cain't go a-traipsin'. Reckon I could talk you folks into lettin' me have one of them empty crates to fill up and take back with me?"

"We'll fill it up and send it back by train," Alisa decided. "That way the Widow Hendricks can have whatever she needs on hand, and you won't worry about leaving." She swished the fan again and sighed. "How can I possibly be so tired? All I've done is sit around all day."

"That's a sign you need to be abed." Lovejoy got to her feet. "Like it or nay, that's just the fact." She walked over and eased Ginny Mae's head onto the blanket they'd spread on the ground near the garden and reached down to help Alisa up. "I'll go get Alisa situated. Miriam, think you could start lunch? 'Lilah cain keep an eye on these here lassies. I worry lest a snake slithers up on 'em whilst they sleep."

"She's never seen you toss your knife, Delilah," Alisa teased.

"I'll see to lunch." Miriam headed toward the main house. "Alisa, you lolly-gag and dawdle."

"I can't bear just lying around while you all work."

Miriam laughed. "You did the hard work and made me rest when I carried Caleb. Now the shoe's on the other foot."

"What foot?" Alisa muttered.

Delilah glanced down at Alisa's hem. Her face went taut for a moment, then she shot Lovejoy a quick look. "Alisa, you're not making this easy. We want Lovejoy to fuss over you instead of finding more to do. The woman never rests."

"Best you start a-prayin' for forgiveness after telling that falsehood, Delilah." Lovejoy waggled her finger. "I niver slept like I do here. Why, I'm like a queen in that fancy above-the-ground bed!"

"If a bed makes a woman a queen, then why am I barefoot?" Alisa looked down then made a wry face. "I can't see my feet."

A few minutes later Lovejoy set a basin

down on the floor and guided Alisa's feet into it. "Soakin' in that water'll cool you off and holp the swollin' go down."

"That's what Titus said last night. He's taken to washing my feet at bedtime." Alisa got teary-eyed. "He said Jesus served those He loved by doing the same thing."

"You got yourself a fine man. Loves you. That's a blessing beyond words."

As Lovejoy lifted Alisa's feet onto a towel in her lap, Alisa whispered thickly, "I'm worried."

Lovejoy looked up at her. "I niver saw the right in fibbin' to reassure folks. I'm not pleased with how yore farin', and that's a fact. I aim to put you abed and keep you there."

"Will my baby be okay?"

"God willin'."

"Titus left last night."

Daniel's blood ran cold at Gideon's so-called greeting when he and the girls arrived at breakfast.

Miriam poured coffee in the mugs on the table. "Alisa's no worse, but Titus couldn't bear to wait till this morning to go."

Dan was so sure of his next statement, he didn't even look around to confirm the fact. "Lovejoy's with Alisa."

"I wanna go be with them. We played tea party on Auntie 'Lisa's bed yesterday, Daddy."

Dan hunkered down and held Polly's hands. "Aunt Alisa is sick, and Lovejoy needs to pay attention to her. No more visiting until the baby is born."

Delilah put a dish of scrambled eggs on the table. "How about if you girls paint a picture with me today? We can have Uncle Titus hang your picture up in their cabin so Auntie 'Lisa knows you miss her."

"That's a great idea." Dan pasted on a smile. "You love to make pictures with Aunt Delilah."

"Auntie Miri-Em and Auntie 'Lisa don't make pitchers; they sew." Ginny Mae worked with her hand a moment and held up two chubby fingers. "Miss Lovejoy gots two new dresses tomorrow."

Delilah smiled. "We gave them to her yesterday. Just wait till you see her in them. She's downright pretty."

"Pretty is as pretty does." Polly singsonged the adage.

"Then Lovejoy's beautiful," Miriam said.

Daniel didn't comment, but he had to agree. The woman had a heart of gold. He just hoped her skill would be sufficient for the task that lay ahead.

With Titus gone, the brothers reassigned chores to cover for him. Knowing he needed to keep his hands busy to stay sane, Dan volunteered to do the hardest, dirtiest tasks. Miriam had packed lunches for the men as usual. He had to give her credit — whatever she packed was always tasty and filling. But today he didn't have much appetite. He knew how Titus must be feeling — that sick dread in the pit of his stomach, knowing his wife and child's lives hung in the balance.

After dragging a stubborn calf out of a mud bog at the edge of the creek and wrestling another from a thicket of scrub oak, Dan's patience had been tested to the limit. Logan was no better. He'd gotten thrown from his horse when it got skittish because a rabbit bolted from its warren. By the time they rode in for supper, Dan figured his clothes could stand up in the corner once he shucked them, and he'd best sluice off and change for supper. But first he needed to know how Alisa and Titus were.

Dan caught sight of Titus standing outside his cabin.

"He looks worse than the two of us put together," Logan murmured.

Dan halted Cooper and dismounted. Without saying a word, he stepped in front of Titus and yanked him into a tight embrace.

"Doc's in there with her," Titus said as he squeezed back.

"How long have you been home?" Logan asked.

"About two minutes."

Dan finally eased his hold. He stepped back but kept his hands on Titus's shoulders. Looking him up and down, he growled, "Let's get you cleaned up. No use in your wife seeing you looking as bad as the road you've been on."

Titus didn't want to leave the doorstep, but Dan and Logan dragged him off. None of the usual brotherly teasing filled the air. Five minutes later, with Titus washed up and wearing clothes he borrowed from one of his brothers, Dan walked him back to see what the doctor had to say.

They'd barely made it back to the porch when the door opened. The doctor came out, and the look on his face made Dan's heart drop to his knees.

"We'd best speak in private," the doctor told Titus.

Titus shook his head.

"I'm sorry. There's no hope for me to save both of them. You have to decide who you want to save. I can perform a cesarean tonight and save your wife, but the child's too small and won't survive. Women with this syndrome can worsen in a matter of hours. If she grows worse, she won't pull through. You can wait and . . . ahem . . . rescue the baby on the slim chance that your wife can last a few more weeks."

CHAPTER 17

Lovejoy stepped outside and took in the situation in a single glance. The doctor's bleak silence, Titus's shocked pallor, and Dan's face lined with determination and grime as he braced his brother's arm.

"Titus, Alisa sent me out here. She knows the baby won't survive if the doctor operates tonight. She won't allow that."

"Doc," Titus said, "there's got to be another choice."

When the doc gave his head a single, decisive shake, Dan rasped, "He loves his wife. They can have other kids."

"Not necessarily."

Lovejoy wrapped her arms around herself and noticed how Daniel bristled at the doctor's curt response. Clearly, he shared her horror at the man's complete lack of compassion. She tried to fish for vital information. "Doc, I know each day makes a powerful difference. How much longer would Alisa have to carry the babe afore it'll have a fighting chance?"

He shrugged. "May as well be two years as two weeks. You don't just need time; you need a miracle."

"We believe in the God of miracles." Dan spoke the words with a certainty that took Lovejoy by complete surprise. "Titus, this is your call. I'll support you in whatever you decide, but if I had things to do over again, I would have done a lot more praying."

Titus heaved a sigh. "How soon do you need an answer, Doc?"

"Morning's as long as we can wait."

"Dan'l, the doc's gotta be hungry as a three-legged wolf. Think we could take him on over for supper? I'll come along for the prayer and bring back a plate for Titus. That way he and his missus cain have a few minutes alone."

They went to the main house where Miriam and Delilah had a meal waiting. Gideon said a heartfelt prayer.

The doctor piled food onto his plate and groused, "I don't see any use in this woman using any of her herbal remedies. They haven't cured the malady."

Lovejoy didn't argue with the sour-faced stranger. To her surprise, Daniel did.

"Alisa's hanging on. That says plenty to

me about how well Lovejoy's treatment works."

"I can't pull a miracle out of my medical bag. I don't know why you bothered to come get me if you believe she can." The doctor shoveled another bite into his mouth. "Then again, nothing's going to make her condition any worse than it already is."

"Paul, there's hawthorn by the mercantile. Cain I send you to town to fetch me some?" The uncertain look on his face forced a smile from Lovejoy. "I'll show you a picture in that book you bought me. I cain tell you 'zactly where it is, so you don't have to fret on whether you picked the right thing."

"Doc, you look like you could use some rest," Logan said. Bryce nodded. "You can bunk down in our place."

Lovejoy couldn't decide whether the Chance brothers truly believed she'd pull Alisa through this crisis or if they were just so angry at the doctor's heartless attitude that they were banding together to keep him at bay.

She brewed black haw bark that she had traded for back home to make a tea and handed the cup to Delilah. "You go pour this down her. I'm out to fetch dandelion leaves and valerian."

"Miriam, will you watch my girls?" Daniel

stood up. "I'll carry the lantern for Lovejoy."

"Oh, Lord, please holp us."

Daniel stood by Lovejoy and wondered what happened to the calm she had displayed until now. She'd knelt to dig up some dandelion and suddenly burst out with those words. She didn't stop there, either. An intercessory prayer poured out of her.

Daniel knelt, cupped her close, and sheltered her from the cold of night. He set down the lantern and reached to hold her hand. When her prayer ended, he haltingly added his own plea. "God, it's been so long since I came to You. I'm asking a lot of You — to forgive me for being so headstrong and stubborn. And please heal Alisa. Lord, spare my brother the grief I've known. Protect their baby. Give Lovejoy the wisdom and stuff she needs to do Your work. In Jesus' name, amen."

Lovejoy looked at him with tears glistening in her big eyes. "Guess since we asked the Almighty to do His part, we best get busy and do our share."

The next morning the doctor reassessed Alisa. "I don't know what you gave her, but the herbs have helped Mrs. Chance to some degree. Her swelling's gone down, but she's still in poor condition. I can't stay here while you dither. Either I operate or I leave."

Titus wavered about what to do. He spent a few moments in privacy with Alisa then came out. "Doc, Alisa won't let you operate. I can't betray her wishes any more than I can give up on either my wife or my child. Sacrificing one for the sake of the other — I can't do that."

Doc left, muttering about how he didn't know why they bothered him in the first place.

Daniel wound his arm around Titus's shoulders. "You've made the only decision you could. We have faith in the Lord, and Lovejoy's been blessed with a healing touch. We'll take it one day at a time."

Dabbing the pencil tip on her tongue, Lovejoy frowned at the paper. She struck out yet another line with the moistened pencil lead. Many of the herbs she needed didn't grow here, or if they did, it was the wrong time to harvest them. White's Mercantile didn't carry a supply of compressed dried herbal cakes, so she was sending a telegram back home.

At three dollars for ten words, she struggled to compose the briefest message possible. No matter how she tried, what she needed couldn't be phrased in ten words. *I never noticed how many herbs have two-word names.* Red raspberry, black sampson, and lady slipper alone took up a total of six precious words. Was Virginia bugle-weed two words or three? She tapped the pencil on the page and sighed. Up to nine words at that point. Then came bethroot, false unicorn, peach bark, and yellow dock. *Delilah has fennel growing in her garden. Blessed thistle, too. But I'll need marshmallow. Cain't use rye ergot on Alisa, but I might need it for Delilah. . . .*

"Lovejoy?"

She jumped and turned around. "Dan'l! Does Alisa need me?"

"No, Titus is with her. I've never seen you scowl. What's wrong?"

"Miriam tole me to write up a telegram so's I cain have Widow Hendricks send essentials. I'm parin' it down best as I cain. White oak bark's available here. So's butcher's broom, dandelion, and rose hips."

"Hold on." He took the paper from her and joined her on the bench. Their arms brushed.

Lovejoy didn't want to scoot away. Since the day he'd found her crying and lent her his warmth and strength, she'd sensed a profound shift in him. He wasn't so caught up in his sorrows that he was oblivious to anyone else. Papa never was one to pay any mind to a female's feelings, and Vern — well, Vern never cared one bit how she was. Plenty of times she'd seen other men support their womenfolk; she wasn't Daniel's, but he'd cupped her head to his sturdy chest, and suddenly the burdens she'd been carrying didn't feel half so heavy.

And here he was again.

He studied the paper, took the pencil, and circled all the things she'd struck out. "Stop fussing and order everything you need. Ask for plenty. With Delilah also in the family way, you ought to have a generous supply."

"This is already nineteen words!"

He shrugged. "Make it forty — even sixty. I don't care about the cost; I want my brothers' wives well. Money in the bank's no good without loved ones to share it with." With that, he handed back the paper and smiled at her — smiled!

He walked off, and Lovejoy was glad he did. She didn't think she could hide her amazement. *Why, Dan smilin' is nigh unto bein' a genuine miracle!*

In the end her telegram ended up being thirty words — a nine-dollar, thirty-word telegram. No one in Salt Lick would believe such extravagance. "Lord, if Thou art of a mind to bestow miracles, Dan's perkin' outta his sorrow is right fine. Might be Ye did that jist to keep from listenin' to me yammer on 'bout him, but I been burdened for him. Whilst Thou art at that miracle business, if'n Thou wouldst protect Alisa and her babe, that'd be wondrous fine."

God listened. They took things one day at a time. Things remained touch and go, but Alisa didn't worsen. Casting a quick look back at Alisa as she napped, Lovejoy prayed the herbs would arrive the next day. *Widow Hendricks'll either figure Alisa's in grave condition or that I've gone 'round the bend, but either way, I hope it makes her shake a leg and send the stuff.*

Delilah quietly tacked Polly and Ginny Mae's latest drawings up on the wall for Alisa to appreciate. "How much longer before the medicines come?"

"Best I cain guess, the packet ought to arrive next day or so," Lovejoy said in a low tone. "Train from back home to San Francisco took five days. Stage to here took another day."

"Paul sent the telegram the day you wrote it, so I guess it just depends on how long it takes your Widow Hendricks to gather up what's needed."

Lovejoy nodded. She still couldn't believe the telegram she'd sent. She drew closer to take a gander at the girls' colorful pictures. "You got them having a right fine time with those fancy Farber colored pencils. Drawin' alongside you is a dreadful treat for them."

"They miss you." Delilah gave her shoulder a nudge. "I'll stay here. You can go on outside for a while. You can play with them or go have a little time to yourself."

Stepping outside Alisa's cabin, Lovejoy heard children's laughter. Miriam was hanging clothes on the line, and the girls were chasing chickens about the yard. The instant they spied Lovejoy, they cried her name and ran to her.

Nothing ever felt half as precious as the way Daniel's daughters flung themselves into her arms as she knelt down.

"Howdy, Daniel Chance."

"Mrs. MacPherson." He nodded at Tempy. In hopes that the things Lovejoy ordered might have arrived, he'd mounted Cooper and was heading toward town.

Her eyes lit at him calling her by her married name. Atop the sorrel mare he'd seen Lovejoy use, Tempy tilted her chin up the road toward Chance Ranch. "I aim to go pay a call on my sister."

"She went off on a walk with my girls."

Tempy smiled. "You sure are nice to share

your lassies with her. Fills in some of the ache in her heart."

"Because she misses her husband?"

Tempy let out a mirthless laugh. "Vern Spencer wasn't worth the cost of the copper pipe he paid Pa for her."

"Your father sold her?"

Tempy folded her arms across the pommel as pain flickered across her features. "Yes, he did."

Daniel frowned as Lovejoy's words echoed in his mind. *Them girls don't know how lucky they are to have a daddy who holds 'em close in his arms and in his heart.* He couldn't fathom what Tempy had just admitted. "What was your father thinking?"

Tempy paled and got a stricken look on her face. "Forget I said anything."

Daniel regretted his outburst. "I didn't mean to alarm you. Whatever happened wasn't your fault."

Her jaw lifted. "It's over and done with, and it's none of your business."

If he hadn't seen the tears sparkling in her eyes, he would have mistaken her resolve for stubbornness. Daniel couldn't let it go. "I'm making it my business."

"Nothing but hurt will come from you digging into my sister's past, Daniel Chance. Best you leave things alone. She's built herself a life again, and I won't let anyone hurt her."

He sat there and weighed his words carefully. "Your sister matters to me. I wouldn't hurt her — ever. It tears me apart to think your father treated her that way."

"What do you mean, Lovejoy matters to you?"

"I care for her." He paused. "A lot." The admission didn't come easily, but he knew from the guarded look on her face that he had to be more forthcoming. "I care enough that I've discussed it privately with one of my brothers."

Tempy's eyes widened. "Really?"

Daniel smiled wryly. "I'm not sure who's more surprised — you at the news or me for confessing it."

"Are you declaring your love and intentions, Daniel Chance?"

"It's not like when I fell in love with my Hannah, so I can't say it's true love." He let out a long, slow breath. "Time will tell, but I can tell you this much: I hold a deep tenderness and respect for her."

"Better you're honest about that and taking time to be sure than that she gets her heart broke." She studied him at length. "Lovejoy hasn't told you a thing about her husband, has she?"

"No."

"I'm going to trust you, Daniel. I'm not sure why."

"It's because you want your sister to have the same happiness you've found." He relaxed his grip on his reins.

She nodded. "That would be a grand miracle."

"So tell me." He fought to keep an angry edge from his voice as he bade, "Start with why your father sold her."

CHAPTER 18

"Pa needed the copper and sugar. Lovejoy was sixteen, so he reckoned he could get a bride price and not have to feed her anymore."

Aghast, Dan stared at Lovejoy's sister.

"Pa ran — runs — a bootleg still. It broke down, and he needed the copper tubing to make it work again. That and four pounds of sugar. He traded his firstborn daughter for them."

Daniel dreaded asking, but he had to. "Did her husband treat her any better?"

"Worse. After she lost the babe —"

His mind reeled. Daniel held up a hand and blurted out, "Lovejoy had a child? She's never said —"

"No." Tempy stayed silent for a moment then sighed. "Almost seven moons into the carrying, Lovejoy came down sick, and Vern was off somewhere. He'd take off for weeks at a time. She was all by herself when she lost the babe." Tears choked her voice. "It was an awful time."

Daniel wiped his hand down his face as if it would clear the horror from his mind. Lovejoy loved babies. She'd been alone and lost her very own.

"When Widow Hendricks said Lovejoy couldn't have more children, Vern tried to sell her back to Pa."

"He didn't deserve Lovejoy or any of her children."

"I agree. Might be wicked of me to say, but I thought about dancing on that man's grave for what he did."

His grave. Lovejoy was a widow, and that fact took on a whole new significance. Daniel felt a small spurt of satisfaction and relief. "He died. When?"

"Four years back."

Daniel's brow furrowed. "She got married at sixteen."

Tempy didn't make him ask. "My sister's twenty-four. She put up with Vern Spencer for four long years."

Four years of a horrible marriage. The thought staggered him. Scrambling to reassure himself things had gotten better, Dan nodded. "So after he died, Lovejoy apprenticed herself to a midwife?"

Tempy clamped her lips together.

His heart wrenched. Lovejoy had endured so much, yet Daniel sensed there was more bad news.

"Lovejoy didn't wait that long. Once she buried her own babe, she went to Widow Hendricks and learned her healing ways in order to be there for other women so they wouldn't be alone in their times of need." After a pause, she added on quietly, "Even when those women were having babes Vern Spencer fathered."

What was a man to say in response to such a revelation? Dan wanted to bellow in anger that Lovejoy had endured so much.

Uneasily shifting in the saddle, Tempy wiped away tears. "I shouldn't have said anything. It was wrong of me."

"No, Tempy. I needed to know."

"Lovejoy never talks of it. Please don't say anything to her."

"Everything you've said was in confidence. You have my word."

"Don't even tell her you saw me." Tempy gulped in a noisy breath. "I'll just go visit another day." He no more than nodded, and she turned the mare and raced back toward the MacPherson spread.

Lovejoy. Daniel kneed Cooper toward town. What an incredible woman. Life battered her, but she'd come through with a sunny attitude and an open heart. Admiration for her filled him.

The first time they met, she'd been singing. Since then she'd had a kind word for everyone.

And she wasn't one just to talk. The woman jumped in with both feet and helped in countless ways, always with a cheerful heart. Just last week Bryce remarked that if she was any busier, she'd have to be twins.

The thought of Lovejoy patiently tending Alisa took on a whole new significance. She alone knew the loss Alisa might face, yet she kept her own experience a secret so Alisa wouldn't have more cause to worry. Lovejoy bore the burden of that worry in complete silence. Her courage humbled Dan.

Suddenly, the words he'd said to Lovejoy as she did laundry weeks ago shot through his mind. *If all it took to make your grief go away was a couple of prayers, then you must not have loved your husband the way I loved my wife.*

He groaned aloud at the memory of those words. What kind of man would be uncaring and unfaithful to his bride? Instead of being cherished, she'd been treated like chattel. Her marriage was a nightmare, not a dream.

How could I have known? Lovejoy always finds the good in people and appreciates everything around her. She never acts as if she ever walked through the valley of the shadow of death. Every hope a woman held dear was taken from her — the babe she carried, the ability to ever bear another one, the love of a mate, the simple dignity of being treated with respect. . . .

Beneath her practical, capable exterior, Dan knew Lovejoy had the tenderest of hearts. How could she deliver other women of her own husband's children? How did she stand seeing them day in and day out? Marriage brought her nothing but humiliation and heartbreak, yet she'd overcome it.

The truth hit him. *I've been so caught up in my sorrow, I kept looking at my loss. I never stopped to thank God for the blessings I had.*

"Lord, You gave Hannah and me three happy years of loving one another. The girls, Father — You gave me two daughters to cherish. I've been lost in grief, but it never occurred to me that the very depth of that sorrow showed how deeply You'd blessed me. Lovejoy talks about rainbows, and all I saw was the rain. Help me to look up."

Cooper whinnied and cantered by a clump of yellow flowers. Mustard, one of the many plants Lovejoy used to heal others. She was like those flowers — sunny and turning her face toward heaven all the day long. What was that verse? The one about mustard seed . . . faith just the size of a mustard seed was enough to move a mountain.

Dan determined then and there to exercise his faith. His mountain of grief had already been shifting and crumbling. Lovejoy told him days ago that she'd hold him up to Jesus. *Well, I'm going to do that same thing. I'm going to hold her up to You, God. I'll have faith that You can heal the hurts in her heart.*

The children and Miriam were perking along right fine. Now that Delilah was over her morning sickness, she'd bounced right back, too. If only Alisa were doing as well. Lovejoy was doing her best to keep Alisa and that wee babe fine.

Daniel went to town yesterday and came back without the things from Salt Lick. No one said a word about it. They all felt the tension, but yammering over it wouldn't change a thing. Today Daniel hitched up the buckboard and took Miriam, baby Caleb, and the girls to town with him. It would be a nice outing, even if the shipment hadn't come yet.

Please, Lord, let it come. Alisa's squeakin' by one day at a time. Each day is a gift, but

214

*we're all so worried. Keep her and that babe
in the palm of Thy hand and rock 'em tender-
like.*

"Lovejoy?"

"I'm right here, Alisa." Dipping the rag in
the pan of water and wringing it out,
Lovejoy made sure she wore a serene expression. "The heat sappin' you, honey?"

"You're just as hot as I am." Alisa pushed
back a russet wisp of hair. "I'm worried
about Titus."

Instead of filling the cabin with chatter,
Lovejoy quietly sponged off the pregnant
woman. Experience had taught her folks
would talk when they were good and ready.

"One of the things I love about him is how
he always sings or whistles . . . or hums."
Alisa's smile didn't reach her eyes. "He's
stopped."

"A gal in this condition's supposed to lie
in a hushed, dark room. Your man's probably trying to be quiet on account that he
loves you and wants to do his part."

"I'm afraid that if the baby and I don't
pull through, he'll end up brooding like
Daniel."

"Then let's pray on that. I'm a scrapper,
and you gotta fair bit of fight in you. Betwixt
us and the heavenly Healer, I'm a-plannin'
to dandle your babe on my knee by the time

215

you and me get Delilah through her birthing."

"You always say the right thing."

Lovejoy chuckled softly. "Wish I felt thataway. Listenin' to you Chance gals talk, I
always think on how wondrous fine you
sound. I'm a plainspoken hillbilly woman,
and I niver heard genuine ladies' conversation till I got here. My words are like grains
of sand on pasteboard, and every word trip-
pin' off yore tongues is like diamonds and
silk."

"In Matthew, Christ said, 'Out of the
abundance of the heart, the mouth
speaketh.' You have an abundant heart,
Lovejoy."

"See there? That's what I mean. Now
here. Time for you to have another cup of
this tea." After her patient emptied the cup,
Lovejoy grinned. "Now afore we pray, I
gotta tell you something wondrous fine
since you mentioned Dan'l's brooding
nature. You've been laid up and not seen it,
but he's a-climbin' out of that dark sorrow.
The man's got a smile, after all."

It wasn't long before Lovejoy saw Daniel's
smile again. The buckboard pulled into the
arnyard, and moments later she heard
eavy footsteps. Though they left the door
pen for fresh air, she'd hung a midnight

blue blanket inches from it to block out the light. In cases like this, light wasn't good for the mama. Sunlight flooded the cabin, then the blanket fell back in place, leaving Daniel standing there. His smile lit the whole place.

"This came for you." He set down a box and pulled the bowie knife from his belt. A flick of his thick wrist, and the twine fell away.

"Thankee, God!" She scurried over and knelt by the box. Lifting the lid, she added, "And thankee, Dan'l. 'Twas good of you to go fetch this."

"How is she?"

Lovejoy cast a look back to assure herself Alisa was sleeping again. The sedative in the tea seemed to be working well, but she'd used the very last of what she'd originally brought in her satchel. "With prayer and all these yarbs, we got a fightin' chance now. This here's lady slipper to keep her sleepy and calm. The honeysuckle'll draw off the swollin'. My, my. Widow Hendricks sent hawthorn for Alisa's headache, even though I didn't even ask for it."

Relief flooded her as she tucked the packets and vials into her apron pockets. "If'n you send Delilah or Miriam here, I'll go to the kitchen and start brewin' up what all we need."

Three days later, even with all the medicinals she'd requested on hand, Lovejoy worried. She knew she needed a bit of time to collect her thoughts and calm her nerves. If Alisa lost the baby, it would be a terrible tragedy — one that Lovejoy related to all too keenly.

I need to take time to shed my own woes, or I'll only add to Alisa's anxiety. The Good Book says a cheerful heart doeth good like medicine. Believing that proverb, Lovejoy left Titus at his wife's side, fetched her dulcimer, and went to sit on the bench at the bend in the creek.

Having tucked the girls into their bed, Daniel stepped outside. Soft music carried on the breeze. Lovejoy was playing her dulcimer, and it was a mighty pretty tune. It didn't take but a second to surmise she'd gone out to that bench he'd made for her by the creek.

Congratulating himself for having thought to make more than just one bench, Daniel started walking. He figured he'd go sit a spell and listen. If Lovejoy wanted privacy or an opportunity to think over a difficult matter, she'd not be making music.

Taking the nearest bench and dragging it

closer, Dan motioned to her to keep playing and singing. Her brows rose in surprise, but she continued as he plopped down. The last lines of "He's Gone Away" faded into the night air.

"You out for a stroll after makin' sure yore lassies are snug as bugs?"

He nodded. "It's nice to see you catching fresh air. Much as you like being outside, it must be making you chafe to be confining yourself to Alisa's side."

"She's the one who's plowing the rocky field." Absently, Lovejoy plucked a few strings. Soon the notes to "Lorena" hovered in the air.

Hannah had loved that song. She'd hummed it now and then as she straightened up their cottage. The memory made him smile — he'd forgotten how he'd teased Hannah about the fact that she followed the biblical injunction to make a joyful noise all too well. Then, too, she hummed because she couldn't ever keep the words straight if she kept on key as she sang them. The memory brought him pleasure instead of pain. *Almighty Lord, thank You.*

The last measure trembled in the air. "What are you going to play next?"

Lovejoy's right shoulder hitched. "Don't have anything particular callin' to me. You have a tune or a hymn on your mind?"

"Hmm." He thought a moment. "What about 'Rock of Ages'?"

She nodded and found her fingering, then started singing. Dan noticed her voice quavered slightly on the second verse. "Let's sing that verse again."

"You'll be a-singin' with me?" Her eyes widened.

He started singing, and she joined in.

"Not the labor of my hands
  Can fulfill Thy law's demands;
Could my zeal no respite know,
  Could my tears forever flow,
All for sin could not atone;
  Thou must save, and Thou alone."

Lovejoy's hands stilled. "I ken the hymn's about salvation, but 'tis fitting for Alisa's situation. No matter what I do, Dan'l, 'twill be Jesus who decides whether to save or take her."

"I know." He leaned forward. Resting his forearms on his knees, he managed to be at eye level to her. In the dim evening light, he could see the glistening tears. "But we're thankful for all you're doing, and we're relying on the Rock of Ages."

CHAPTER 19

A thin wail shivered in the air. Daniel held Titus back. "Half an hour. You agreed to Lovejoy's rule."

"I'm not waiting. That's my wife and babe!"

"And you owe them both to God's grace and Lovejoy's skill. There are medical details she needs to tend to in there."

Titus groaned. "I'll credit God for Alisa and the baby making it. I'm thankful for all Lovejoy's done, too. But that ax . . ."

Daniel folded his arms across his chest. "What's wrong with my ax? I like to think it helped."

"It's hillbilly nonsense. Putting your ax under the bed didn't cut Alisa's pain."

Though he secretly agreed, Dan goaded his brother to delay him from bursting into the cabin. "Of course it did. I just sharpened it."

Paul started chuckling. "It's one thing to

be crazy about a woman; it's another thing to be plumb crazy."

"Fine." Dan smirked. "When Delilah's in labor, I'll take my ax and go chop wood."

Paul snorted. "You'll be lucky if she doesn't swipe it and keep it under our bed from now until our baby comes." He poked Titus. "Notice Dan didn't deny that he's crazy about Lovejoy."

Titus kept craning his neck so he could keep the door to the cabin in view. He grumbled, "She's dead set on going back to Salt Lick. If she doesn't let me in there in the next five minutes, I'll personally stick her on the next stage out!"

"You can't mean it." Paul glowered at Titus. "Delilah's going to need a midwife."

Daniel rocked back on his heels and shot his brothers a smug smile. "I aim to coax her to stay forever, but Delilah's a good excuse in the interim."

Titus jolted. "Forever? Dan, are you saying —"

Dan jerked Titus around. "The door's open!" *Whew. I hushed him up just in time.*

"Titus, yore family's a-waitin' to greet you." Lovejoy beamed as she stood there. Miriam slipped on out, and Titus raced in. Lovejoy stepped out and closed the door to allow them a moment of privacy.

"Well?" Dan prompted.

"Mother's a tad weakly and the child's smallish, but I estimate they'll both be right as rain within a week."

"What is it?" Delilah rushed over, holding both Daniel's girls by their hands.

"It's a baby," Polly said with certainty.

Dan chuckled and looked to Lovejoy for the answer. "Boy or girl?"

"Cain't say. 'Tisn't my news."

"It's a girl, Daddy." Ginny Mae shimmied up his pant leg like a bear cub climbing a tree.

"How do you know that?" He wound his arm around her and planted a noisy peck on her sun-kissed cheek.

"Auntie 'Lisa sewed gowns, not pants," Polly explained.

He tweaked her nose. "Baby Caleb wears gowns, and he's a boy. All babies wear gowns."

The door opened once again. Titus stepped out into the morning sun and beckoned them in. "Come meet Tobias!"

Lovejoy waited as everyone else hastened to see the baby. Dan wrapped his free arm about her shoulders and walked her to the door. "Tobias, huh?"

"It means 'God is good,' " Titus explained.

"And He is," Dan agreed.

Everyone admired the baby and said sweet things to Alisa. Dan didn't like how she looked at all, and he was more than glad Lovejoy planned to stay and attend her. After a handful of minutes and plenty of praise, Lovejoy shooed them all out and told Miriam, "I'd count it a favor if you'd fetch me them jars I made last night of the Virginia bugle-weed and the black sampson teas. Alisa needs to drink them now."

Dan lagged behind. As she nudged him out the door, he whispered, "Yell if you need help."

She nodded.

His gaze held hers. "You're something else, Lovejoy Spencer. Without you, Alisa and Tobias wouldn't be here."

"That's God's blessing, not my doin'. He listened to yore prayers."

"I'm talking to Him plenty these days." Daniel barely kept from adding on, *And often it's about you.*

A week later Lovejoy sat on the beautiful red and gold Turkish rug in Alisa's parlor. She and the girls played with dolls while Alisa and Miriam both nursed their sons in the bedroom. Delilah sat on the settee, sipping Lovejoy's special raspberry-lemon tea after hanging dozens of diapers on the clothesline.

"One, two, free, seben," Ginny Mae counted.

"One, two, three, four," Polly corrected in an exasperated tone.

"I's playing on the floor, so I don't have to say it."

Lovejoy tickled their cheeks with the tails of their braids. "The both of you are getting grumpy. Naptime."

"Do we get a tea party when we wake up?" Polly's eyes lit with hope.

"Are you offerin' to pick the pine needles and wash 'em up?"

The girls' braids danced as they nodded emphatically. On the way back to their cabin, both girls filled their little hands by stripping a fistful of pine needles from a low bough. Lovejoy had them rinse the needles in a pie tin she kept by the pump. "Now that'll do us just dandy. Pollywog, see if'n you cain spy a rose hip. We could add that in."

Delighted that they'd helped, the girls galloped into their cabin, took off their gingham aprons, and scrambled onto the bed. In a matter of moments, they fell fast asleep.

Brewing the tea took hardly any time, but Lovejoy tried to get everyone to have either berries, something lemon or orange, or this tea each day. Pine needles and rose hips contained that same component as citrus and kept scurvy at bay. The pungent taste didn't much appeal, so she took to adding a wee bit of blackstrap molasses. Not only did it sweeten the drink, it also built up blood.

"Yoo-hoo!"

Lovejoy raced out of the cabin. "Tempy!"

"We come callin'," Eunice said as the sisters hugged. "Wanted to see the new babe."

"He's a grand little man-child." Lovejoy gave the three visitors a stern look. "Alisa's still catawamptiously chewed up. Best you all sing yore praises short and sweet. We cain visit more out by the bend in the crick."

Mindful of Lovejoy's edict, Tempy, Lois, and Eunice oohed and aahed over little Tobias, then came back out. Miriam accompanied them and promised to keep an eye on Polly and Ginny Mae.

As the MacPherson women settled on the benches by the creek, Tempy sighed. "We hoped we'd be taking you home with us today. I miss you."

"It does my heart good to see you, too. I been busy here, but thangs ought to settle down in another few days. I'll come back to the MacPherson spread, leastways till Delilah's child arrives. Even then, y'all are fairin' well. I aim to traipse back over here every couple of days and lend a hand."

"We understand," Lois said. "Day'll come, one of the Chance women'll come bail us out."

Tempy grabbed Lovejoy's hand and squeezed it. "Even if they never end up setting foot on our spread, we'd still want you to help them."

"Aunt Silk is fit to be tied," Eunice blurted out. "We got us a letter Asa Pleasant writ for her. She said you promised you'd stay with us."

Lovejoy added on, "Until I got you settled. I'd never promise more than that. Salt Lick won't have a healer if'n I stay here."

"Widow Hendricks is doing fine," Tempy argued.

"Widow Hendricks is spry of mind, but her back and joints won't let her go on much longer." Lovejoy shook her head. "This don't bear no chatter. Facts is facts. Now let's us not waste our breath or time on that when you cain tell me 'bout what y'all been doin'."

They had a lovely visit, and when it was time to leave, Eunice and Lois decided to scamper ahead and peep in on the baby once more. Tempy lagged behind.

"It does my heart good to see you lookin' this happy." Lovejoy needlessly smoothed her sister's collar. "Aglow — that's what you are. Aglow with love. God be praised."

"And you!" Making a sweeping gesture, Tempy continued, "Scrumptious as a peach in that new dress and a ribbon to match." She waited a beat then added, "Seems Daniel's name tripped off your tongue quite a bit today. Are you falling in love?"

"Temperance MacPherson! What kind of nonsense is that?"

"He's the kind of man you can ride the river with."

"I'm not getting into the marryin' boat! I'm fixin' to go home, and I'll thankee to remember that."

After her sister left, Lovejoy sat back down on the bench and stared at the sunlight sparkling on the creek. Daniel Chance was a fine man. As Widow Hendricks would say, "a man you cain tie to." *Well, he is that steadfast and dependable. Goodhearted. God-fearing. But just because he's a man a woman could tie to doesn't mean I'm tying the knot with him. Like he said at the wedding — he's had him a bride already. He don't have a heart for marryin' up again.* She sighed heavily. *Don't reckon I need to think on it, anyway. I promised to go back home.*

228

But the thought of leaving him left her close to tears.

CHAPTER 20

"Could you hold still a moment? I'm getting seasick watching you bob up and down."

Lovejoy let out a throaty laugh and pinned another diaper to the clothesline. "Got two babies here, each using a dozen of these a day. Better you get seasick than drown!"

Dan nudged the laundry basket aside with the toe of his boot. "I heard you're thinking of going back to the MacPhersons', but I'd like to discuss an alternative."

"Go ahead and talk." She scooted around him, bent, scooped up a diaper, and reached for the clothesline again. "Might be, you ought to close yore eyes if'n I make you dizzy. Weather's a-shiftin', and I want these dry afore them clouds take a mind to sprout leaks."

"I've been thinking —"

"Think to tell Polly not to get her sister wet over at the pump."

Dan glanced over his shoulder. "Polly, cut it out and get away from there. Ginny Mae, step back. The last thing we need is for you to have muddy shoes."

"What's the first thing we need, Daddy?" Polly shouted back.

He gladly took that question as a segue. Hooking his thumbs through belt hoops, he looked at Lovejoy as he called back, "We need Lovejoy to stay and mind you girls while I deliver cattle to Fort Point. I want you girls to behave so I can ask her."

Lovejoy finally stopped working.

Polly and Ginny Mae dashed over. "Ask her, Daddy! Ask!"

He cleared his throat. "Mrs. Spencer, I'd —"

"You said you was askin' Miss Lovejoy, Daddy." Ginny burst into tears and grabbed hold of Lovejoy's skirts. "I want Lovejoy."

She stooped down and gathered the girls into her arms. "It would take a hardhearted woman to turn down a plea like that."

Daniel dared to reach over and slide a single fingertip down her cheek. "And you've got the softest heart of anyone I've ever met. You'll stay?"

"I'm honored you trust me with your treasures."

Daniel walked off feeling quite smug. His

plan couldn't be working better. Day by day, week by week, he was going to court her with all the reasons she should become his wife. Lovejoy understood this message loud and clear: He trusted her with his beloved daughters. What better thing could a man tell a woman than that?

Covers rustled. The soft, wet sound of Ginny Mae sucking her thumb in her sleep. Polly mumbled a few garbled words, and Lovejoy smiled. Even in her sleep, Polly couldn't stay silent. With Daniel gone, Lovejoy could have slept in his cabin and left the connecting hall doors open so she'd hear the girls if they cried out, but she didn't. Accustomed to a pallet on the floor, she slept each night close by them just to relish these sweet sounds.

During the day she missed seeing Daniel. And his brothers, too, Lovejoy belatedly added. Except for Titus, who stayed behind and couldn't stop smiling and humming. Having a strong, protective provider around was a novelty — not, she hastily reminded herself, that Daniel was her man. He was just, well . . .

No use hoping or dreaming his attention and help were caused by anything more than the fact that the other Chance men were involved with their wives and babes. It was natural that Dan and she became friendly on account of her minding his lass-ies.

At nighttime Lovejoy filled her heart with the simple things mothers took for granted — how each of the girls said "amen" with such certainty at the end of bedtime prayers, the extra tight hug around the neck one last time before lying down, the way tiny toes curled under on a cold floor the next morn-ing.

"Lord, Thou blest me with those gifts early on when I had little sisters. 'Specially my Tempy. I reckon I didn't appreciate them then, and I'm sorry. I 'spected I'd have a passel of young'uns and would relish it all then. This time I know it's just a few nights, but I'm gonna fill up my heart with this."

She drifted off to sleep and woke the next morning to warm little knots of knees and elbows on either side of her. Opening her eyes, she whispered, "What is in my bed?"

"A Pollywog." Polly giggled.

"Pollywogs are wet little critters. I'm hop-ing yore not wet."

"I not wet, Miss Lovejoy." Ginny Mae wiggled around and trapped Lovejoy's braid beneath herself. "I a big girl!"

"Yes, you are. Dumplin', you're a-layin'

on my hair. Since you got plenty of yore own, what say you let me have mine back?"

Asking Ginny Mae to move was akin to asking the ocean to have a tide. The child was in motion all the day long. No longer trapped, Lovejoy turned onto her back and gathered the girls in her arms. "How did I get me a pair of lassies?"

"We snuck," Ginny Mae boasted.

"Daddy told us we could." Polly sounded quite proud. "He said you might be scared, sleeping somewhere new. We're 'posed to make you not be a-scared."

"And you done a fine job." She lay there and fingered the scalloped texture of their braids. *Dan'l did the selfsame thing those nights when they got so sick.*

"Do we getta go on the gathering walk this morning?" Polly's upturned face lit with hope.

" 'Course you cain. It's like I get to carry sunbeams with me when you come along."

Funny how something could become a habit in just a few days, Lovejoy thought as she tied Ginny's little blue gingham apron. Being a make-believe mama felt so right. Never one to be overly fanciful, Lovejoy reminded herself this was just a fill-in week, a pretend time. Once Daniel made it back, she was going to go back to live at Tempy's.

But I'm going to love every minute of this while I cain.

"Polly-my-wog, fetch me the brush. Yore hair looks like a haystack gone sidewise."

"Daddy says my hair is pretty as a princess's. Soft and light as a moonbeam."

"Just like Mama's," Ginny Mae tacked on.

"Then yore mama must've been comely as a china doll." Lovejoy took the brush and got busy. She'd gone through this routine each morning now. The first time, surprise speared through her that Daniel spoke of his wife to his daughters. He was always so closed-mouthed about that. By the third day, she understood it was a father-daughter ritual. For just a moment today, Lovejoy felt a pang of jealousy. Hannah had wed and loved Daniel and cherished these sweet babes. *Oh, what I wouldn't give to have been blessed like that.*

Practicality took over. *If'n Hannah hadn't been blessed like that, I wouldn't be a-havin' my turn with these girls now.*

Once dressed, Lovejoy put on her sheath and slipped in the knife as the girls claimed their pails. Somewhere along the line, they'd each been given smallish lunch buckets. Before the walk was over, Ginny's would be dragging on the ground. That didn't matter. She looked adorable, clutching it in her chubby hand. Lovejoy slipped the edge of her gunnysack under her belt and stepped out into the morning, thrilled by the feel of a little hand in each of hers.

"Good mornin', Lord!"

Dirty and bone weary, the Chance men headed for home. Normally the married ones pushed to reach home right away; the single ones took an extra day or two of freedom. This time Daniel led the pack to get home.

"You'd think someone was holding a lit match to Cooper's tail the way Dan's racin' ahead," Paul teased.

It wasn't the first time Daniel had taken the brunt of some ribbing on this trip. He didn't mind, either. Fact was, he'd forgotten how good it felt just to hear a baby's first cry, to tease his brothers, to enjoy simple pleasures. In the past few months, life had turned around. He didn't have to haul himself out of bed in the morning. Lovejoy was right: Starting off by greeting each day and asking the Lord's guidance made all the difference.

Each of the men had a bedroll tied to his saddle, but the two horses that carried supplies on the way to Fort Point now bore packs with things the men had bought in

San Francisco. Imagining Lovejoy's delight at what he'd gotten for her, Dan rode on.

When they reached the ranch, Gideon and Paul both vaulted out of their saddles and swept their wives into whirling hugs. Dan dismounted and immediately had a daughter wrapped around each leg. Lovejoy remained in the vegetable garden and simply waved at him. In the past this reception had felt empty — he'd keenly suffered Hannah's loss. This time he didn't mind. With the certainty of a man who'd found his mate, Dan knew the next homecoming he'd have Lovejoy in his arms.

After the men had taken long, hot baths and eaten a savory meal, the Chances remained around the table. Gideon started by handing a paper-wrapped parcel to Alisa. "Titus placed this order. Hope it's all right."

Alisa murmured her thanks, opened the package, and let out a cry of delight as a sand-colored, merino wool shawl spilled into her lap. "Oh, it's so soft! Thank you!"

Miriam and Delilah both accepted dresses from their husbands with voluble delight.

Polly and Ginny Mae tore the paper off their package: a new children's game called Snakes and Ladders. Eager to play it right away, they danced about while Titus read the instructions and Delilah arranged the pieces on the board.

While they were occupied, Daniel put a package in Lovejoy's arms. She gave him a stunned look. He grinned. "Go on ahead. Open it."

"It's for me?"

"Of course it is."

She looked bewildered. "Ain't niver gotten a present afore."

"Then it's well past time." He motioned for her to get started. The fact that she'd not experienced such simple delights bothered him. Daniel promised himself then and there that he'd make up for all the birthdays and Christmases she'd done without.

Lovejoy painstakingly unknotted the twine, wound it about her fingers, and tucked it in her pocket. "Cain use that later." Likewise, she unfolded the paper carefully. "This here paper's enough for letters and envelopes for months to come."

"Hurry, Lovejoy. We wanna play our game!"

Lovejoy gasped as the burgundy leather satchel came into view.

"When I fixed the latch on your other satchel, I noticed the tapestry was getting frayed." Daniel said the words in a low tone.

She ran her fingers over the beautifully

tooled leather. Tears glistened in her eyes, turning them molten, and a beguiling pink suffused her cheeks. Looking up at him, she said, "Thankee, Dan'l. 'Tis enough to steal my breath."

"I knew you'd be able to use it."

She nodded. "When I go back home, it'll remind me of you."

When I go back home. When I go back home. The words echoed in her mind as Lovejoy tried to fall asleep in the above-the-ground bed back in the room she shared with baby Caleb. She flipped over and stared at the rafters. Admitting to herself that lying here was useless, she dressed and went for a walk. She ended up out on her favorite bench by the bend in the creek.

"Lord, I'm in terrible trouble here. Terrible. I'm needed back home. Widow Hendricks cain't last long, and it's just plain wrong to leave the folks in Salt Lick without a healer. When I started learnin' my yarbs, I pledged to Thee that I'd minister in Thy name and touch in Thy loving care. Well, far as I cain see, that sends me right back home.

"Only it don't seem like home no more, God. That's the problem. Well, that's part of the problem. See, my heart's here in Reliable. Tempy's gonna end up in the family way and will need my holp. Mama put her in my care long ago, and now it's not feelin' right to leave her. And the other folk here, they need my holp, too.

"And bein' dead-level honest, Father, somewhere along the line, I done lost my heart. Dan'l is a fine man — and I love him. I know he's not interested in me for more than a friend; that's a sore spot, but I reckon I cain settle for that. It's plenty more than I ever had. His daughters are a joy, and he's needin' holp with 'em.

"It's nigh unto tearin' my heart in twain. I need to go, but I'm a-longin' to stay. Thou knowest best, but I'm beggin' you to ease my heart and mind so I cain do what's right. Amen."

"We've taken a vote," Daniel announced at the breakfast table the next morning. He gulped down a bite of Delilah's incomparable flapjacks and stared at Lovejoy. "You're to stay here."

"It wasn't just the Chance men who voted, either." Miriam held Caleb in one arm while drizzling syrup on Ginny Mae's flapjack.

Logan groused, "Women voting. What's the world coming to?"

240

"It makes sense for you to stay," Daniel continued, ignoring his brother. "You've filled that loft with all sorts of stuff. Folks come here for you when they need assistance."

"And we love having you here." Alisa cradled Tobias close to her bosom. "You've made all of the difference."

"Now hold yore horses. God makes the difference — not me. I'm nothing more than a plain, old hillbilly woman with a knack for usin' yarbs."

Daniel studied her from the top of her shiny, fawn-colored hair down the length of her peachy dress. "Only a blind fool would call you plain or old."

"So it's settled," Bryce cut in. "You'll stay here."

"I'll think on it."

An hour later, Bryce shouldered Daniel. "She'll think on it. I'm trying to decide whether that's a good or a bad thing."

"We have time. She promised to stay until Delilah has her baby. No use rushing her. I'm going to sneak into her heart one step at a time."

"We come to fetch ourn." Obie MacPherson's comment rumbled through the barnyard. Eunice sat beside him on the buckboard and nodded.

"Lovejoy is settled in nicely here," Miriam protested.

"She belongs with her kin."

"Now, Obie," Delilah reasoned, "we all understand she's Tempy's sister. You have to admit, the women of both families have been doing plenty of visiting back and forth."

Lovejoy felt Ginny Mae and Polly clutching her skirts.

Obie turned his gaze on her. "I pledged to Mike that I'd fetch you back. Your place is with kin. Tempy's setting up a place in the first cabin. You cain put all your healin' stuff there. Folk'll learn to come call for you there if'n they's a-needin' holp."

I prayed, Lord. I asked Thee to let me know Thy will. Thou art taking me away from Daniel. Thou art taking me away from these girls. Give me grace to do this.

She squared her shoulders. "I'll pack up."

CHAPTER 21

"Gone?" Daniel roared the word in disbelief. He stomped into his daughters' cabin and looked upward at the loft where Lovejoy kept her healing supplies.

Empty. Not a berry, scrap of bark, leaf, or vial remained. His heart felt just as empty.

"You was supposed to make her stay," Bryce said from the doorway.

"I'm sure she'll come visit," Miriam soothed.

Dan didn't bother to hide his glower. "What do those sneaky varmints think they're doing, dragging her away from us like she's some kind of pup and they get the pick of the litter? She's a woman — my woman."

"Yes, but —" Miriam began.

"I'm getting her back."

"We'll watch the girls for you," Delilah volunteered.

"Nope. I'm taking them with me. She can't resist them."

Miriam planted herself directly in front of him. "You're doing nothing of the kind."

Dan lowered his voice. "Miriam, I loved your sister, and I was a good husband to her. Hannah's passed on. It's no insult that I've fallen in love again."

A bittersweet smile lit her face. "I've been praying you'd find happiness, Dan. I don't begrudge you that at all. It's just that though Lovejoy loves Polly and Ginny Mae, you don't want her to think you're after a nanny. Either you go on your own, or you shouldn't go at all."

He gave her a quick hug. "I'll bring her back."

The stool teetered beneath her feet as Lovejoy reached to hang a bunch of leaves.

"Obie pounded them up there for you, hisself," Lois said as she handed up another bunch.

"It was shore clever of him to bend them so's they make hooks. It's right handy."

"Tempy tole him to put in lots." Eunice stayed over by the stove and took out a loaf of bread. "Obie started funnin' her, on account it's gonna look like a dyin', upside-down garden in here."

"But it all smells so good." Tempy inhaled deeply.

"That's my cookin', not the plants and such."

Lovejoy forced a smile. The easy companionship and contentment at the MacPherson spread was an answer to so many of her prayers. God had graciously blessed the gals and settled them into loving marriages. In truth, that's what Lovejoy had asked of the Lord when she set out on this trip.

I got no business, askin' or wantin' anything more.

". . . pintail ducks and pheasants. They had themselves a great time."

"Hmm?" Lovejoy realized she wasn't keeping up with the conversation.

"Chances took down as many as our men. Smokehouses are gonna be full unto bustin'."

"That's the last of it," Eunice called up. "Got every last thing put away now."

"A letter came for you, Lovejoy." Tempy helped her big sister hop down from the stool and gave her the folded paper.

Running her fingertip over the edge of the page, Lovejoy smiled. The spidery script brought back pleasant memories of Widow Hendricks writing labels to paste on jars and vials. Wheat flour, a pinch of salt, and water mixed together made the paste for those labels, just as it sealed the carefully folded edges of the letter. No one back home used fancy stationery and envelopes like the Chance women did.

"Widow Hendricks sent all sorts of yarbs on Alisa Chance's behalf," Lovejoy said as she carefully coaxed open the paper. "And the Chances holped me gather and send back a whole crate in return."

"That's fitting," Lois said. "What with her spinebone being so twisty, she prob'ly won't be able to keep up on stock."

"I know." Lovejoy sighed. "I'm frettin' over how thangs are back in Salt Lick."

"You promised you'd stay for Delilah's birthing." Tempy gave her a startled look. "You won't go back on your word."

" 'Course not. I aim to get busy and gather up sufficient for Reliable and Salt Lick, though."

Eunice started laughing. "Get busy? You cain't sit still any sooner than I cain catch a weasel asleep."

Lovejoy sat on the stool, one foot on a rung and the other on the floor, since the silly thing rocked a mite. She read silently — partly because Widow Hendricks might tell her something private about one of their patients and partly because the outspoken old crone didn't mince words when she spoke of others. Some things didn't need to be passed on.

Dear Lovejoy,

That box came in right handy. Them mule's ear roots work grand on Otis's rheumatiz. Mine, too. Send more if'n you cain spare them. Had the Pleasant young'uns gargle with yore kind of slip elm and healed soar throt right quik. Other than that, folk are chipper as cain be. Mayhap we cain trade boxes of yarbs now an agin.

Which is why I writ this. Lots of prayer wint into this, so listen with yore heart. Tempy writ and said there's a widower there with two lassies. You been holping his kin, and she tells me the both of you got on real good. He sent telegrams. First one tole me the whole story in just a few words. "Lovejoy needed. Difficult maternity cases. Request you continue serving Holler."

Then and thar, my heart tole me the truth. Yore needed there, and I'm needed here. May be, 'tis just yore talent they need. Silk Trevor has conniptions whenever she thinks on you leaving her gals. Yore sisters are keeping watch on your pa, but Tempy's there, and she'll need you to deliver her babes as the years roll on.

Parson preached on Titus last month bout old women holping the younger gals. He brung Hattie Thales to me that week.

Hattie Thales. Lovejoy bit her lip. At thirteen, she'd been married off to a man twice her age. She'd lost a babe halfway through the carrying three times in a row. A deadwood fell in a stiff wind and half crushed her man a year back. She'd tended him till he passed on just before Lovejoy left to come here.

Nobody wants Hattie. She cain cook and clean, but a man wants sons. I took her in. We been in yore house, and she's got a clever mind. Learnt yarbs on our first walk and recited them back the next day. I got me a few good years yet to train her up, and this'll give her a happy life.

'Tis yore nest, but I'm fixing to push you out. Less you say otherwise, me and Hattie'll keep serving Salt Lick, and you cain serve God where He sint you.

You been like a dotter to me, and I will

alwuz holt you in my heart.

Fondly,
Willomena Hendricks

Lovejoy stared at the letter. Tears blurred her eyes. *Heavenly Father, I've been a-prayin'. Even afore I knew how much I wanted to stay here, Thou wert makin' it possible. It near takes my breath away. About Dan'l, Lord —*

"What's a-wrong?" Eunice gave her a stricken look.

"Bad news from home?" Tempy bustled over and wrapped her arms around Lovejoy.

"No. No, it's not." Lovejoy tried to blink back the moisture and carefully fold the letter on the same creases to keep it in good condition. She didn't dare look up, else Tempy would read her face just as clearly as she'd just read these words.

"Ever'body's okay?" Lois asked. "Aunt Silk?"

"Widow Hendricks said folks are fine." *And for the first time in my life, maybe things will turn out fine for me, too.*

"That's all?"

Lovejoy wanted to go off on her own. Think. Pray. Hope and dream.

Eunice tugged on her sleeve. "More's gotta be happening than that."

"Well, yes." Her voice quavered as the

realization of God's provision washed over her anew. "She's taken to training up Hattie Thales."

"Hattie!" Tempy jolted upright. "Who would have imagined that?"

"Her man was sick a good long while. I swan she's good at handlin' sick folks." Eunice nodded.

"But nobody's half as good as you, Lovejoy." Lois wiped her hands on her apron. "You got the healin' touch. Don't be sad. Folk's are always gonna seek you first."

Tempy let out a squeal. "This means you can stay! You won't be going home!"

Lord, Thou hast shewed me Salt Lick ain't home anymore. Thou hast been a-changin' my heart and mind all this time.

"You belong here," Tempy chattered on. "Obie, Hezzy, and Mike have been champing at the bit to bring you back from Chance Ranch. This here cabin's to be yours."

"See?" Eunice beamed. "Yore sister's right. You belong here."

"No, she doesn't," a deep voice said from the doorway.

"Now ain't that a fine howdy-do." Eunice gave him a sour look. "Our Lovejoy's been a-workin' her fingers to the bone for yore kin and —"

"Eunice, hobble your mouth," Tempy said, nudging her away.

"I'd like to speak with you." Daniel directed his words at Lovejoy then cast a meaningful glance at the others. "Privately."

Lovejoy slipped off the stool.

Tempy stepped in front of her big sister. "She'll be out directly."

"If she wants to," Lois tacked on, then rudely shut the door in Daniel's face.

Daniel stood there and grinned. He'd grown up with five rowdy brothers and knew that stubborn, protect-our-own look. Well, he'd let them have one last time to do it, because after this, Lovejoy was going to be his.

Minutes passed.

Daniel scowled. He could hear soft murmurs from the other side of the door, and he started considering the possibilities of either banging on the door or eavesdropping at the window. *What's taking so long?*

The door opened, and a woman stood there. For a moment he barely recognized Lovejoy. It was her, all right, in her peachy-colored dress. But her eyes and red nose tattled she'd been crying. And her hair — the MacPherson women all standing behind her had messed with her hair. Instead of her customary plait that danced along her spine or slipped over her shoulder and hung to her waist, they'd taken out the braid and twisted sections and pinned them into a cameo-sort-of look.

A virulent rush of red flooded Lovejoy's face, and she slammed the door shut again.

Dan shoved it open and plowed past Eunice and Lois, who clucked like a pair of upset hens, to get to Lovejoy. She stood in the center of the cabin, back turned toward him as she tore out the hairpins. He stepped behind her, stilled her hands, and murmured, "Let me."

One by one, he slid the pins from her hair and let them ping on the plank floor. Tempy patted his back, then she and the others scooted out the door. Lovejoy shuddered as he pulled out the last pin.

Forking his hands through her hair, he purred, "That's more like it." He crushed the thick waves in his palms then combed his fingers through the length. "There. Better."

She sidestepped and yanked her hair over her shoulder. Quickly dividing it into three portions, she muttered, "Couldn't convince them. No use trying to prettify —"

He pressed his fingers over her mouth. "You're right."

She tried to blink away moisture in her eyes.

"There's no use trying to prettify a woman who's already perfect."

Beneath his fingers, her lips parted in shock. He brushed his thumb across her lower lip. "I planned to take the months until Delilah had her baby to court you. I thought I had plenty of time to take things slow and easy."

"Court me?" Hope flickered in her eyes.

"But I'm not about to be separated from you — not even by a single fence. I'm taking you home with me. Today."

Suddenly, all the color in her face drained away.

Daniel chuckled and wrapped an arm about her waist. He'd shocked her speechless.

Lovejoy shook her head. Tears started to seep down her face, yet she leaned into him.

Daniel wouldn't figure out what was going through her mind, but something told him these weren't tears of happiness. He was sure of his feelings for her. *Did I speak too soon? Rush her when she needed that slow courting? Maybe that time was more important than I knew after her father and husband treated her so badly.* "Sweetheart, if you just want a little time —"

Despair filled her voice. "It cain't be."

"Anything's possible when you love someone." Whatever the problem, he'd solve it. Daniel refused to let anything come between them.

Pain flickered across her face.

"Salt Lick Holler doesn't need you like I do. To the depths of my soul, I swear that's the truth."

" 'Tisn't that at all. Widow Hendricks is trainin' up a new gal to holp."

He glided his hand along her neck and slipped his fingers into her hair until he cupped her head and tilted her face up to his. "Then stay here. Be my wi—"

"No!"

Daniel stared at her in stunned silence.

She tried to pull loose of his hold, but he held her fast. "What's wrong?"

"Yore offerin' me every dream I could ever have, but I cain't give you what you deserve." Her face crumbled and anguish filled her voice. "Men want sons."

"Sons? What does that have to do with me loving you?"

"I'm barren, Dan'l." The confession left her sobbing. "Widow Hendricks . . . Hattie . . . men and sons."

Broken words poured out of her broken heart. Daniel couldn't stand it. He dipped down and pressed his lips to her mouth to silence them. For a moment, she clung to him, then she tried to push away.

"Shhh." He held her tight.

"I won't ask you to sacrifice —"

"I want a wife, not a brood mare." He tilted her face up to his. "I want you, Lovejoy. I love you."

"But sons," she moaned.

"With five brothers, Chance Ranch is bound to have plenty of boys running around. We already have Caleb and Tobias. Even if they're the only ones, we can hire help. I've got you, and I've got my daughters. I'm more than blessed."

"You really feel that, Dan'l?"

His lips hovered a breath away from hers. "I lost my heart to you."

Wonder and hope lit her features. "It really don't matter to you?"

"The only thing that matters is, God brought us together."

A soul-deep sigh shuddered through her, and she cuddled close. "Truly, Dan, I love you."

"Be my wife."

"Yes." She barely whispered her breathless assent, and he pressed his lips to hers.

The very next Sunday, Daniel pulled Lovejoy into his arms and kissed her again.

"Daddy, you're 'posed to do that after Parson Abe tells you to. It's at the end, not now," Polly scolded.

"I can't believe it's drizzling." Delilah handed Lovejoy her bouquet. Eunice and Lois both picked up Daniel's daughters to carry them into the barn where they always held church during bad weather. As matron of honor, Tempy stooped to gather up Lovejoy's skirts so they wouldn't become muddy on the trek to her wedding.

"I've got her." Daniel swept her into his arms.

"Oh, looky there, Dan'l! We got us a rainbow on our wedding day!"

He stopped in the middle of the yard, looked at the expanse of color, then grinned at his bride. "And it's not one stripe short."

EPILOGUE

Six years later

"So Jesus fed five thousand with just that one little boy's lunch." Lovejoy folded her hands. "Uncle Paul's gonna pray; then you young'uns scamper off to bed."

After Paul said the prayer, the cabin burst into a flurry of nighttime hugs and kisses. The Chance clan now boasted a full dozen children, and Miriam, Alisa, and Delilah all blossomed with the promise of another babe apiece in the coming months.

Lovejoy nuzzled a kiss on Miriam's youngest toddler's cheek then laughed as Bryce and Logan loaded up kids to piggyback them off to their cabins.

Delilah stood next to Lovejoy and said, "I read a verse this morning that fits you."

"Oh, what is it?"

Delilah smiled. "Psalm 113:9 — 'He maketh the barren woman to keep house, and to be a joyful mother of children. Praise ye the LORD.' Your hands have caught all of these kids, and you add so much to their lives. I'm praising God for you."

"Now wasn't that jist the best verse I ever heard? Thankee, Delilah." Lovejoy gave her a hug.

After they tucked Polly and Ginny Mae into bed, Daniel gathered his wife into his arms. "I was watching you again this evening, and something struck me anew."

She hugged him back. "What was that?"

"Your name — how fitting it is. You brought love and joy back into my life."

She stood on tiptoe. "Praise ye the Lord."

ABOUT THE AUTHOR

Cathy Marie Hake is a southern California native, who loves her work as a nurse and Lamaze teacher. She and her husband have a daughter, a son, and two dogs, so life is never dull or quiet. Cathy considers herself a sentimental packrat, collects antiques and Hummel figurines. In spare moments, she reads, bargain hunts, and makes a huge mess with her new hobby of scrapbooking.

The employees of Thorndike Press hope you have enjoyed this Large Print book. All our Thorndike and Wheeler Large Print titles are designed for easy reading, and all our books are made to last. Other Thorndike Press Large Print books are available at your library, through selected bookstores, or directly from us.

For information about titles, please call:
(800) 223-1244

or visit our Web site at:
http://gale.cengage.com/thorndike

To share your comments, please write:
Publisher
Thorndike Press
295 Kennedy Memorial Drive
Waterville, ME 04901